# AVA'S CRUCIBLE

## BOOK TWO: EMBERS OF EMPIRE

### BESTSELLING AUTHOR
# MARK GOODWIN

# DEDICATION

Let every soul be subject unto the higher powers.
For there is no power but of God: the powers that be
are ordained of God.

Romans 13:1


To the members of Oath Keepers; America's
current and formerly serving military, police, and
first responders, who pledge to fulfill the oath all
military and police take to "defend the Constitution
against all enemies, foreign and domestic."

Thank you for your service and dedication to this
country and for your commitment to your motto,
"Not on Our Watch."

To donate to this worthy cause or for information
on joining Oath Keepers, visit them online at
Oathkeepers.org.

# ACKNOWLEDGMENTS

I would like to thank my Editor in Chief Catherine Goodwin, as well as the rest of my fantastic editing team, Stacey, Glemboski, Jeff Markland, Frank Shackleford, Kris Van Wagenen, Sherrill Hesler, Paul Davison, and Claudine Allison.

# CHAPTER 1

And I will bring the third part through the fire, and will refine them as silver is refined, and will try them as gold is tried: they shall call on my name, and I will hear them: I will say, It is my people: and they shall say, The Lord is my God.

Zechariah 13:9

Ava lay motionless on her pillow, her entire body aching. One eye was swollen shut. She opened the other eye to see Charity walk in the bedroom. "What time is it?"

"A little after noon." Charity bent down to clip the leash to Buckley's collar. "But don't worry, I walked Buck this morning, and I'm going to take

1

him out again now. You just rest."

"After twelve? Why didn't you wake me?" Ava grimaced as she slowly sat up.

Charity looked on with a sympathetic expression. "You needed the sleep."

"Did I miss anything?"

"Ross spoke this morning. The networks claimed he was giving his concession speech. It was anything but."

"Oh yeah?" Ava flexed her stiff, swollen ankle and winced.

"He basically said Texas and Florida would hold new elections, and that he'd have the National Guard secure the polling stations this time."

"Don't the state governors have to activate the National Guard?" Ava gritted her teeth as she reached for her crutches.

Charity rushed to help with the crutches. "Not according to Ross. He cited the 2007 NDAA, which expanded the president's authority over the Guard."

Ava gingerly rose from the side of the bed, placing her weight on the crutches. "The Markovich camp is going to sit back and allow Ross to have a new election?"

"The media pundits don't think so, but the Markovich campaign hasn't released an official statement about Ross' claim yet. There's no denying that Antifa's actions swayed the vote in Florida and Texas. The facts are clear."

"Facts have never proved to be an obstacle for the media. I can't see Markovich letting them get in the way." Ava navigated a path to the restroom.

Charity led Buckley toward the front door. "I'll

be right back. Betty saved you some breakfast."

"Thanks." Ava closed the bathroom door. Her stomach sank as she looked into the mirror over the sink. "I look like Quasimodo's ugly cousin."

Her morning routine took three times longer than usual. She delicately washed her face, blotting the water from her swollen eye and split lip. She quickly learned to take the pain of hitting a sore spot without gasping since deep breaths sent searing pain to her cracked ribs. Shallow inhalation and glacial movements were her only defense against the constant torture of her injuries. Eventually, she emerged from the bathroom.

"Good morning!" Betty Hodge stood at the end of the hallway wearing a pleasant and perky expression. "How did you sleep?"

Ava made an attempt to smile with the uninjured side of her mouth. "Fitful. But that's because of my cracked ribs. The accommodations were superb. I put one of the blue towels over my pillow so I wouldn't get blood on it."

"Oh, don't even bother." Betty waved her hand. "Those old things don't matter. Come on into the kitchen. I've got some biscuits and ham waiting for you. How do you like your eggs?"

Ava followed her to the kitchen where a place was set for Ava at the eat-in counter. "Scrambled— if it's no trouble."

"None at all, dear."

Sam Hodge walked in from his study near the front of the house. "Ava, you survived the night. That's a good sign. How are the Steri Strips holding up on your lip?" He came closer and examined her face.

"Still there," she said.

He nodded pensively. "Probably could have used a couple stitches, but you'd been through so much already. Ribs and ankle about the same?"

"Yeah." Ava took her time mounting the bar stool at the counter.

"Hey!" Foley entered the kitchen.

"Good morning." Ava breathed in as she looked him over. He was so cute. She really wished he hadn't seen her all beat up, especially at this early stage of what she hoped might be the start of a real relationship.

He approached Ava and pushed her hair back from her bruised face. He kissed her ever-so-tenderly on the forehead.

Ava looked at the floor. "My face is a disaster."

"You're still cute to me."

"Normally, I don't give much credence to insincere flattery; but I'll make an exception—just this once."

He leaned in for a soft kiss on the lips. "Oh, I'm sincere. Cross my heart."

She looked up to see her father come through the door with her laptop opened. Her heart melted more for him than it had for Foley. His presence represented a lifetime of secret hopes and hidden dreams that she'd told herself would never come true. Yet here he was, in the same room with her.

"Good morning, Ava." Ulysses smiled at her compassionately. "Did you get some rest?"

"I did, thanks. And you?"

"I slept enough. I've been lurking around the

Antifa message boards and social media pages, trying to get a sense of what they'll do next. I borrowed your laptop. I hope you don't mind."

Ava wondered how risky that might be, especially since her father was connecting via Sam Hodge's WiFi. She knitted her brows together. "Is that safe? I mean, couldn't the government track the IP address and confuse us with Antifa?"

Ulysses shook his head. "I'm running the Tor browser and I have an incognito operating system booted on your laptop. So there's no record of anyone ever visiting any of the sites on your machine."

Ava looked curiously at him. "You'd never even seen a modern computer until two years ago. How do you know more about all of this than me?"

Ulysses sat on the bar stool next to Ava. "Computers, cell phones, and the internet frightened the heck out of me when I first came home. I felt like the future had left me behind. It was overwhelming, and I was worried that I'd never be able to catch up. At first impression, it seemed I couldn't function in society without the ability to navigate the technological landscape.

"That guy from the State Department who was helping me re-integrate set me up with a laptop and a smartphone. He showed me the basics. The rest, I learned on YouTube. I got caught up in a matter of weeks. Afterward, I kept going. I wanted to learn all I could about it. For someone who missed nearly three decades of technological advances, it's fascinating."

"Yeah, I guess I've grown up with the internet. I

probably take most of it for granted." Ava felt inspired by this man who had been through so much but not lost his will to live and drive to keep learning.

"I'm sure you heard that Ross is going to have new elections for Texas and Florida."

"Charity told me." Ava nodded.

Ulysses tilted the computer screen for Ava to see. "Antifa is lashing out over Ross' recall. They're targeting your area for more mayhem."

"What do you mean by *mayhem*?" Ava inquired.

Ulysses pointed to the laptop. "The Twitter hashtag is *#BurnItDown*. They've issued a sign amongst their members. Any vehicles or homes with a black 'A' on them will be spared."

Foley peered over Ava's shoulder. "Like the anarchy 'A'. Once again, we have the communists, who want absolute government control, contradicting themselves by espousing the symbol which stands for *no government*. So they posted the secret symbol for anyone to see?"

Ulysses shook his head. "No. I've been active on their message boards and on social media for a few months. I made up a profile to stalk them. I'm a member on one of their forums on Blackbook."

"What's Blackbook?" Betty asked as she plated Ava's eggs with the leftover ham and biscuits.

"It's the darknet version of Facebook," Ulysses answered.

Sam Hodge seemed concerned. "Isn't Tor and all that dark web stuff for criminals?"

"If Markovich has his way, every conservative who owns a gun will be considered a criminal this

January." Ulysses moved the laptop out of the way so Betty could place Ava's breakfast in front of her.

"Thanks, Betty. It looks delicious." Ava began eating while the others talked.

Foley lifted his shoulders. "Truth is treason in the empire of lies."

Sam rubbed his chin, as if the reality of Ulysses' statement was sinking in slowly. "I suppose you're right."

Ulysses watched Ava eat. "If I can borrow your Jeep, I'll go put some A's on your building and apartment door. Black electrical tape should work, and it'll come off easy when the threat has passed. I can grab some more of your stuff, if you like."

"Let me finish breakfast and I'll go with you." Ava forked another bite of ham into her mouth.

"You're in no condition. If we get into trouble, you'll be at risk. I couldn't deal with that." Ulysses shook his head adamantly.

"I'll go with you. I'll drive." Foley offered.

Ulysses stared at Ava for a moment then turned to Foley. "That would be fine." He then looked at Sam. "I appreciate you letting us stay here. It might turn out to be a prolonged event. I'm thinking of getting a travel trailer so accommodations won't be so tight. Would you mind if I keep it here until we leave?"

Sam smiled. "I have no problem with you bringing a trailer here, but I assure you, we don't mind sharing our home for ever how long it's necessary."

Ulysses glanced back at Ava. "It would be good to have options. I've got a trailer picked out."

Ava wasn't sure what her father's financial situation was, but he didn't seem to be strapped for cash. "You guys be safe. Can I still use my computer?"

"Yeah." Ulysses rebooted her laptop and removed a small flash drive from the side. He placed the thumb drive in his pocket and looked at Ava nervously. "Can I get another hug?"

She held her arms open wide. "Sure."

Ulysses was very gentle as the two of them embraced. "I'm so glad I got to meet you."

Ava choked back her tears. "Me, too. I pray God will give us many years to catch up."

# CHAPTER 2

None calleth for justice, nor any pleadeth for truth: they trust in vanity, and speak lies; they conceive mischief, and bring forth iniquity.

Isaiah 59:4

Ava sent yet another text to Foley.

"Still haven't heard back from them?" Charity walked into the Hodges' living room with James at her side.

"Nothing." Ava glanced up from her phone. "Phones are completely overloaded. Texts aren't even going through. I should've had them both sign up for WhatsApp before they left."

"Why would that work if texts aren't going

through?" James inquired.

Ava put her phone down. "I don't know that it would. But it operates on a different network which might not be overloaded. It has fewer users."

Charity took a seat next to Ava. "You said your dad was going to buy a travel trailer. Maybe he needed some stuff for it."

Ava let her head droop forward like a stalk of limp celery. "I finally get a dad and a boyfriend, and they both go missing at the same time. I should have known better than to get my hopes up."

Charity stiffened her upper lip and put her arm around Ava. "Why don't we give them 'til sunset before we start writing their obituaries."

Ava huffed. "Fine. But I should have gone with them."

Charity smirked. "Yeah—you shouldn't even be out of bed today."

"The local news will be coming on." James turned on the television.

Ava looked on more for the distraction than out of concern for what was happening. The swelling around her eye had gone down considerably since that morning, allowing her to see out of both sides.

The female anchor in the newsroom addressed a correspondent in the field. "Porter, downtown Austin looks like a scene from the middle east. It's absolutely unrecognizable—apocalyptic."

Behind Porter were three tan Humvees flanked by soldiers wearing body armor and armed with M4 rifles. On either side of the Humvees, burned-out vehicles lined the streets. Smoke damage crept up exterior walls and plastered over the insides of buildings which could be seen through windows of broken glass. "That's right, Jennifer. President Ross has already begun mobilizing the National Guard to stabilize the so-called problem areas. Of course, the cities where he didn't win are the metropolitan areas which have been labeled *problem areas*."

The newsroom anchor replied. "It does look pretty rough where you're located, Porter. Do you question the president's sincerity?"

Porter shook his head. "Jennifer, our team was right here last night. I know you were back at the station, but just like the folks at home, you saw the same things I saw. The vandals responsible for last night's pandemonium were mostly associated with right-wing extremist groups like Right Now and Oath Keepers."

The female reporter replied, "Those are the people I was seeing in the streets last night as well. But, Ross has put all the blame on Antifa and the Social Justice Warriors League.

"Tell us, Porter. In your opinion, has Ross' dictatorial command to turn the streets of Austin into a police state achieved his goal? Has he put an end to the violence?"

Porter looked over his shoulder. "The troublemakers have dispersed from the downtown area." He turned back to the camera. "But I suspect the order will only serve to disperse the violence into the suburbs. What he has done is silence the voices of the people. SJWLs and peaceful protestors from Antifa have lost their First-Amendment Rights."

Charity looked at James who'd taken a seat on the upholstered chair next to the couch. "Do you think that part could be true? Do you think Antifa will spread out to the suburbs and rural areas to continue wreaking havoc?"

"I'm not sure. I suppose it's possible." James kept his attention on the television.

Just then, Buckley began barking wildly on the front porch.

Ava reached for her crutches. "We need to get our guns, now!"

James jumped up from his seat and motioned for Ava to stay seated. "I'll handle it! You're in no condition for a shootout."

"My trigger finger still works. If trouble is headed our way, I don't want to be lounging on the couch like a sitting duck when they bust through the door." Ava worked the crutches to maneuver herself towards the downstairs guest bedroom.

"Then at least let me help!" Charity hurried after her.

The two girls retrieved their rifles and quickly returned to the living room. James stood by the door with his shotgun in one hand peering out the window. Buckley was still barking.

"What's all the commotion?" Sam Hodge rushed into the room with his pistol in hand.

"Looks like Ulysses bought a truck to go with his trailer. I guess Buckley didn't recognize the vehicle. False alarm." James let the curtain fall back into place and turned back toward the others.

Ava continued on her crutches to the window to

confirm James' report, her rifle slung over her back. "Oh! Thank you, Jesus!"

Sam Hodge let out a sigh of relief. "I suppose that was a good drill."

"Yeah, we should probably each have a firearm on us at all times. At least a pistol. Next time could be the real thing." Ava watched as Foley's truck pulled up behind the travel trailer.

Buckley ceased barking and ran out to meet the vehicles, tail wagging.

She looked closer at the front end of Foley's F-150. The fender and headlight were damaged, as if Foley had been in a wreck. She watched with concerned eyes as he stepped out of the vehicle. He didn't appear to be injured. She continued to monitor the two men as they approached the house.

Her father didn't seem to be hurt either. He carried a black laptop bag over his shoulder. Ava figured that he'd bought his own machine for stalking Antifa.

Buckley followed Foley and Ulysses to the door. Ava gave him a firm pat on the head. "Good job, Buck! You stay outside and keep an eye out for trouble." She looked up at Foley. "Did you guys get in a scrape?"

Foley looked at Ulysses. "A little one. No big deal."

Ulysses offered a reassuring smile. "Yeah, no big deal. Antifa was trying to block the road when we left Austin. Foley gently nudged them out of the way."

Ava noticed that neither of them was carrying any of her stuff from the apartment. "Were you able to go by my place?"

Foley lowered his brow and looked at Ulysses.

Ulysses put his hand on Ava's shoulder. "It's gone. Your building is just a burned-out shell."

Ava wished she'd brought more stuff. She had her most important belongings, but she'd never had a chance to go through all of her adoptive mother's things. Her clothes could be replaced, but she regretted not selecting a few keepsakes from her mom's belongings.

"I'm sorry, Ava," Ulysses said.

Quickly she realized that she still had Ulysses and Foley. She hadn't known either of them very long, but they meant more to her than anything she'd lost. "It's fine." Ava forced a grin and looked up into her father's eyes.

James interrupted, "The news is spinning the riots to be the work of Right Now and Oath Keepers. We know that's a lie, but they said the National Guard moving into Austin might push the melee into the more rural areas. Could that mean Antifa is headed our way?"

Ulysses turned to Foley. "We drove by a group causing trouble out by Bee Creek."

Foley nodded. "Bee Creek is still a pretty good distance from Paleface, but it wouldn't hurt to be prepared."

Ulysses looked at Sam. "We should assign a watch schedule and come up with a plan to defend the property."

Betty Hodge joined the pow wow. "A watch schedule? Sam, what's happening?"

"It's just a precaution." He put his arm around

her. "They saw trouble out by Bee Creek. We need to be ready if they come this way."

Foley said, "We should put a couple guys out by the road; make them real visible. If we look like a hard target, Antifa will pass us by and find somebody else to pick on."

Ulysses shook his head. "It's a good theory, but I don't think it's the best call for our situation."

"What do you suggest?" Sam asked.

"Antifa is looking for trouble. If we tell them this is the place to find it, they'll send in a huge force to squash us.

"In the Art of War, Sun Tzu said to appear weak when you're strong. I recommend we let them think we're unprepared. If anyone comes looking, we draw them into a kill box and eliminate them before they can call for help or give away our location."

Foley crossed his arms. "Sun Tzu said to appear weak when you're strong and to appear strong when you're weak. I'm familiar with his writing. Compared to Antifa, we're weak."

Ulysses nodded. "That's true, but we won't be up against Antifa. We'll only be dealing with a small recon team at best. With us in fortified positions having predetermined fields of fire, we're much stronger than a small raiding expedition."

"I disagree," Foley stated. "You and I are the only experienced shooters."

"They can all fire a weapon," Ulysses replied.

"But they're not trained."

Ulysses paused then looked up at Sam. "It's your home, and ultimately your decision."

Sam tucked his pistol in his pants pocket and

rubbed his lower jaw in contemplation. Finally, he turned to Ava. "What do you think?"

"Me?" Ava did not want to be pitted against Foley or her father in this debate. "What do I know?"

"You're quick on your feet; always have been. Anytime something comes up at the office, you figure it out. I've watched you for years. You don't give yourself enough credit."

Ava looked at Foley and Ulysses; she considered the two proposals. "Antifa is ruthless and sneaky. I think if they saw guards posted out front they'd pass by and send people back through the woods later— taking out the guards from cover. Sorry, Foley. I have to agree with Ulysses on this one." She turned to her father, "I meant to say *Dad*."

Foley straightened his back. "Then I'll fully support Ulysses' plan. Let's put it together and get some basic tactics training going."

"Thank you," Ulysses said. "Sam, may we use your study?"

"Absolutely." He nodded.

Betty held her hands up. "Can we figure out how we're going to fight World War Three after we eat dinner?"

Ulysses cracked a smile. "That's the best idea yet."

# CHAPTER 3

He teacheth my hands to war; so that a bow of steel is broken by mine arms. Thou hast also given me the shield of thy salvation: and thy gentleness hath made me great.

Samuel 22:35-36

Ava sat on the foot of Foley's bed in the upstairs guest bedroom. She pretended to shoot her AR-15 at hostiles outside of the window. "Bang, bang, bang."

"Okay, you're empty. Change mags." Foley instructed.

She repeated the motion of ejecting the spent magazine from her rifle and replacing it with a new one from the bag around her shoulder. As she'd done before, she attempted to pick up the empty mag.

"Leave it," Foley said. "If you live through the gunfight, you can go get your mags later. If you don't, you won't need them anyway. But you don't want to take your eye off the enemy to pick up magazines."

"Okay." She nodded.

"Let's do it again."

"Again?"

"Yeah. This is important. When people are shooting at you, your heart will be pounding and you'll be shaking like a leaf. If you've changed magazines a couple hundred times, muscle memory will take over. Otherwise, the extreme stress of the situation may keep you from being able to perform the very rudimentary task."

"Alright." She ran the magazine-change drill four more times, using up the remaining magazines in her bag.

"Good job." Foley collected the empty mags laying around on the floor and placed them back in the bag.

"I didn't thank you for not being mad at me."

"For what?"

"Picking my dad's plan over yours. It was nothing personal."

He chuckled. "I know that. You made a rational choice. If I got mad at you over that, I wouldn't deserve you." He leaned in for a light kiss on the side of her mouth that hadn't been split open in the attack.

Thursday morning, Ava awoke early. She looked on the floor next to her bed for Buckley, but quickly remembered he'd been assigned a permanent position as official guard dog on the front porch. Once again, she felt stiff from her injuries, but the swelling in her face continued to subside. Charity remained asleep, so Ava reached quietly for her crutches. She tucked the clip-on holster of her Glock 43 onto the waist of her sweatpants before exiting the bedroom.

Ava's ability to move noiselessly on her crutches improved rapidly. She closed the bedroom door without waking Charity. Ava checked the window before opening the front door. Buckley rushed to her side. "Good morning, Buck! You kept the bad guys away all night. Good boy!" Ava leaned against the door frame to bend over and pet the dog. She moved cautiously to the stairs, lowering herself to sit down and spend some quality time with her pet. "Hopefully, this will all be over with soon, and you'll be back in the house with the rest of us. But for now, just know we appreciate it."

Buckley seemed content with the attention he received from Ava. He put his head on her leg and lay next to her on the porch. Ava relaxed on the porch for half an hour. Her mind drifted and she found herself praying, asking God for protection and pleading for the safety of those with her; especially Ulysses and Foley. Afterward, she kissed Buckley on the head and went inside. He begged to come in with her. "I'll be back, Buck. And I'll bring you something really good to eat."

The smell of fresh coffee permeated the inside of

the house. When she reached the kitchen, she saw her father sitting at the counter. "Good morning. How did you sleep?"

"Good morning. I didn't yet. How about yourself?" Ulysses looked up from the laptop.

"I slept like a log. I let Dr. Hodge—I mean Sam, talk me into taking something a little stronger for my ribs and my ankle. Pharmaceutical reps were always bringing in samples to the dental office, so evidently, he has a pretty substantial stockpile of painkillers and antibiotics."

Ulysses poured her a cup of coffee. "Those things could come in handy."

"Thanks." She leaned her crutches against the wall and sat down on the bar stool where the coffee cup waited for her. "Why didn't you sleep? I thought Foley and James were supposed to take turns for night watch."

Ulysses nodded. "They did but I stayed up all night keeping watch from the window above the garage. We've got no reliable form of communication other than our cell phones. We're running walkie-talkie apps on our phones, but the app drains batteries like crazy. And if we don't have cell service or WiFi, the app doesn't work. So, that's my mission for today. I've got to get us some radios."

Ava sipped her coffee. "Where are you going to get radios?"

"Good question." Ulysses scanned the screen of the computer. "Vandals hit the shops of the Galleria and broke into homes as far out as Falconhead last night. I'm trying to find an outdoor shop or big-box retailer who is still open around here."

"Falconhead? That's not far from us."

"Nope, which makes it all the more important that we're able to communicate."

"Did you try the small towns going away from Austin?"

"No. I'm not sure they'd have what we need."

"Marble Falls is probably only twenty miles from here. I doubt they're getting much fallout from Austin. I'm sure they have a Walmart, and probably one of the big-box home improvement stores. Do you think a place like that would have walkie-talkies?"

Ulysses searched the map on the computer. "Probably won't have the best radios, but beggars can't be choosy."

"I'll ride out there with you if you want. I can't imagine we'd have trouble out west."

"Maybe not, but we could run into problems on our way back. I think it would be best if you stayed here."

"Sure." Disappointed, Ava looked down at her coffee mug.

Ulysses hesitated as he put his hand on her back. "You don't know how bad I want to take a car ride with you; to sit and talk, and hear about everything I've missed over the last twenty-nine years. But I need you to be safe. How about if I pick up a couple of fishing poles while I'm out? One day this week we can drop a line in the river behind the house; just you and me."

Her eyes brightened. "That'd be great."

"Mornin'." Sam took a coffee cup from the

cupboard.

Ulysses looked up from the computer screen. "Good morning."

"Good morning, Doctor," Ava said.

"Remember, it's just Sam 'til we get back to work." Hodge smiled.

"Right." Ava nodded. "That's going to be a tough habit to change."

Sam filled his cup and walked over to look at Ava's face. "Swelling is almost gone. You'll probably have some discoloration for a while. Your lip might start itching too. But don't pick at the Steri Strips. They need to stay on for a few more days. Did the pills help you sleep?"

"Yes, thanks."

"Good. But leave the pills alone during the daytime. You need the pain to remind you to stay off that ankle until it can get better."

Betty Hodge entered the kitchen. "I bet the pharmaceutical reps would have crossed you off their route if they heard you talking like that."

Sam furrowed his brow. "Dentists, doctors, psychiatrists; the entire industry makes it too convenient for people to pop a pill every time they have a bad day. If somebody is in serious pain, they need medication, but my colleagues in the medical field have helped to create the most over-medicated society on the planet. Eighty percent of the world's opioids are consumed by Americans who make up 4 percent of the global population. The US is also the top consumer of antidepressants."

Charity came into the room, wearing her robe. "It's not going to be a pretty picture if we have a prolonged civil conflict and all those people can't get their meds. I'm the one who gets to hear Dr. Hodge's patients calling asking for a refill on their Vicodin or Percocet. If they're still in that much pain, Dr. Hodge wants people to come back in the office to see if they have an infection. You can tell who the abusers are because they always get upset at being inconvenienced. Even though we don't charge for a follow-up visit, they never come back in." Charity filled her coffee cup and started another pot.

"Does everyone like pancakes?" Betty asked.

"I do, but I'm going to have to decline this morning." Ulysses stood up.

"Oh?" Sam sipped his coffee.

"I'm going to head out to Marble Falls; try to locate some radios."

"I'll ride along if you don't mind waiting until after breakfast," Sam said.

"Thanks, but I want to hurry so I can get back and have the radios ready to use for tonight's security watch."

Betty took out a mixing bowl and the dry pancake mix. "Sam, you were supposed to help me with the garden today. We need to get some more vegetables started in case this thing goes on for a while."

"I can help you with the garden," Charity offered.

"You should take Sam with you." Ava's face showed her concern.

Ulysses said, "I'd love to have you come along, Sam. But I do need to get moving."

Sam chugged his coffee. "Then I guess I'll tag along. We'll eat when we get back."

"It won't take but five minutes to whip up a stack for you men. Eat something before you go. I'll make ours after you boys get on the road."

"What do you say?" Sam glanced at Ulysses.

"Okay." Ulysses' lips were tight, as if he had a deep sense of urgency. But, he didn't seem willing to risk offending his hosts.

Ava asked her father, "Can you show me how to navigate the Deep Web? I can't help in the garden or do much else, but maybe I can lurk around some Antifa message boards and pick up some intel."

Ulysses nodded. "That could be more helpful than you might think." He opened the Tor browser and retrieved a 3-inch-by-5-inch index card from his back pocket. "This is a list of URLs for the sites I've been monitoring. The really malicious actors don't use indexed sites. Those web pages typically have a string of random numbers and letters rather than words or phrases for their URLs. And they almost always end in dot onion rather than dot com or dot net."

Ava watched as he logged into one of the sites.

He slid the computer in front of her. "Just monitor. Don't respond or post questions. I've built a fairly specific online personality for these message boards."

Ava looked at his avatar and screen name. "Harley Quinn?"

Ulysses nodded. "She's a comic book character; supervillain. She was the Joker's girlfriend at some point. A lot of the guys on these boards are computer nerds. If they think they're talking to a female nerd, they'll be more open about sharing information. Harley Quinn evokes a certain sexiness, too. Once they start imagining that they're talking to a hot chick, they get real generous about what they're willing to say.

"The intelligence world has always used attractive female agents to extract information via seduction; honeypots they call them. With computers, not only do you not have to be attractive, you don't even have to be female."

Ava read some of the threads on the screen. "I bet you were really good at your job."

"The one thing I learned in that Chinese prison was that regret is absolute poison for your mind. But on the few occasions that I did allow myself to wonder what it would have been like, I imagined being an electronics salesman or a delivery driver who came home to his family every night after work. I was good at my job, but I wish I could have been good at being a father."

She cautiously put her hand on his. "It wasn't your fault. And God used my adoptive mom to look after me. She gave me a very good childhood. Besides, you're here now, and that's what matters."

"Here's your pancakes!" Betty placed Ulysses' breakfast in front of him.

"Thank you."

Ulysses and Sam finished their food and hurried out the door. Betty made pancakes for the girls, preparing extra in case James and Foley woke up before she and Charity returned from the garden.

Once everyone was out, the house was quiet for Ava. She diligently studied the threads on Blackbook and the various message boards her father had shown her. Any information which Ava deemed to be noteworthy, she jotted down on a pad of paper. She clicked over to the Hidden Wiki page. "Wow, these guys are selling guns, cloned credit cards, passports, counterfeit bills, hacking services, PayPal accounts, drugs; it's the entire black market on one website! I can't believe I never knew places like this existed on the web!" Ava continued to scroll through the darkest corners of the Deep Web.

She paused when she heard Buckley barking. She glanced up but couldn't pull herself away. It was like driving by a car wreck that she wasn't able to turn away from. Buckley barked again. "I'm coming, Buck."

Ava tore her eyes from the computer and reached for her crutches. Buckley's vocalizations grew more agitated. "I said, I'm coming!" Ava worked her crutches to get to the front of the house as quickly as possible. Once there, she looked out the front window to see a blue Honda Civic coming down the drive, in front of a white box truck. "That doesn't look right."

# CHAPTER 4

The Lord trieth the righteous: but the wicked and him that loveth violence his soul hateth. Upon the wicked he shall rain snares, fire and brimstone, and an horrible tempest: this shall be the portion of their cup.

Psalm 11:5-6

Men with black hoodies stepped out of the Civic. Ava counted four, the two from the rear of the car had AK-47s slung over their shoulders. Two more came out of the box truck. Likewise, they wore black hoodies and bandanas. The one from the passenger's side of the vehicle held an AK-47. Unlike the others, it was shiny; stainless steel.

Ava turned toward the stairs and shouted,

"Foley! James! We've got trouble!"

One of the men from the Civic yelled. "Anybody home?"

Ava ignored the call and started up the stairs.

The man called out once more. "If anyone is home, you better come get your dog before I shoot it."

Ava's stomach sank. "Foley! James! Wake up!" She pivoted on her crutches, shaking her head as she went back to the door. She looked out to see that Buckley had pushed the men back to their vehicles.

POW! The spokesman for the group fired one round from a large pistol in the air. "That was my only warning shot. The next one is going in the dog!"

Ava gritted her teeth as she opened the door. "Buckley, come here, boy!"

Buckley continued to bark and growl at the men.

"Buck! Now! In the house!"

Buckley snarled and showed his teeth at the men but reluctantly obeyed Ava's command.

The man asked, "You here alone?"

"No," Ava answered.

He looked at the man next to him. "Really? Other people are here, but they chose to send out the beat-up crippled girl to see what all the commotion was? Put your dog in the bathroom so I don't have to shoot him."

Ava hoped Foley would come down soon. She put Buckley's leash on him.

The men walked up on the porch as if they were going to follow her inside. Buckley began barking wildly again.

"You have to stay outside!" Ava yelled.

The man pointed his pistol at Buckley. "I'm just going to shoot him."

"No, please! I'll put him up!" Ava held Buck's leash as she pulled him to the bathroom. She considered going inside with him, but she was afraid the men would just pepper the thin door with gunfire. Once he was inside, she turned back to the man. "What do you want?"

"We're taking up a collection, for the cause. Thanks to the right-wing lunatics, all the grocery stores in Austin are closed. We need food, provisions, guns, ammo, anything you can spare."

"We can't spare anything," she said defiantly.

"Oh, I'll decide that." Even though his mouth was covered, the lines on the sides of his bloodshot eyes showed his sinister grin.

POP! POP! POP! Two of the men who were standing near the bottom of the staircase fell to the ground. Foley rushed down the stairs firing on the other four.

POW, POW, POW! The man with the shiny AK-47 stepped back out the front door, kneeling behind the door frame for cover as he returned fire.

Foley ran past them toward the kitchen, shooting as he moved. POP! POP! POP! He gunned down one other man before taking cover behind the counter.

The man with the pistol kicked Ava's crutches out from beneath her and grabbed her from behind by the throat. He pulled her to the floor, hiding himself behind her body. "Take it easy. If I die, you die." He held his pistol to the side of her head.

BANG, BANG, POW, POW, POW! An exchange of gunfire went up and down the stairs between the man with the shiny AK and James. The stainless AK dropped to the ground just outside the door. It glistened in the sun as a growing pool of blood ran out onto the porch.

Buckley barked and growled like a rabid dog from inside the bathroom.

Ava's captor called out to Foley and James. "Good shooting, guys. But the fun is over. I've got the girl, and I'll put a bullet in her head unless you do exactly as I say."

Foley yelled, "Okay, let's work this out. I'm putting down my weapon." Foley placed his AR-15 on the floor. He stuck his hand out from behind the counter.

"Good. Come on out, slow and steady." The man pressed the pistol against Ava's temple with the barrel pointed toward Foley. "Let's stand up," he whispered to Ava.

"I can't, my foot!" she protested.

"Suck it up, or that foot is going to be the least of your problems." He stood against the wall and pulled her up.

She winced in pain and cried out in agony. "OUCH!"

"You're fine. Stay cool."

"Just walk away. It's all good." Foley stood with his hands up.

"Not that easy." The man shook his head. "You and the gunslinger up there are going to load up my weapons, your weapons, and all your provisions in that white box truck out there. Me and your little punching bag here are going to drive out to the road. If I don't have any issues, then I let her out."

"You're not leaving with her, and she's not my punching bag. I didn't do that to her," Foley argued.

"Brother, I get it. A man's gotta relax. Whatever. I'm not here to get in your business. But let's just get this over with and we can all be on our way."

Foley replied, "Okay. We'll do what you asked, but she's not getting in the truck with you. Agreed?"

The man looked at Foley. "Just tell your boy to bring his gun down here."

"Not until you agree to my terms. She stays here."

"Okay, she stays here. But no more negotiating. Get him down here now, with his rifle, before I end this."

"James, come on down. Put your rifle on the ground." Foley looked into Ava's eyes, as if to reassure her that they'd get through this.

Ava knew the situation wasn't going to end well. The man hadn't frisked her and knew nothing of her Glock tucked inside her sweatpants. But if he saw her reaching for it, she'd never get off a shot. She'd be dead.

James came down the stairs, still holding his AR-15 at a low ready position. "I don't think this is a good idea, Foley. Once I put my gun down, he can just shoot all three of us!"

Ava's captor acted anxious. "Put it down, or I'll shoot all three of you anyway!"

"Relax!" Foley said to the man, still holding his

hands up. "James, it's fine. Put down your gun."

James looked stressed. His hands were shaking, which made the invader even more nervous. He pointed the pistol at James. "Put that gun down or everybody is going to die."

Ava saw this distraction as her only chance. She held on to the man's arm with her left hand while the other slowly lifted the tail of her shirt. She felt the handle of her small pistol. She pulled it out of the holster.

James' voice became louder and high-strung. "Let her go, and I'll let you go. But I'm not putting down my gun!"

"How about I just shoot you, then?" The man's reply sounded jumpy. "If you take a shot at me, you'll hit the girl!"

Ava felt sick to her stomach. The tension of the moment was more than she could handle. She watched the man pointing the pistol at James. She couldn't see his head, but she could feel his breath against her neck, so she knew about where his face was.

"Last chance, guy!" the intruder yelled right beside Ava's ear.

"No! Everybody just calm down!" Foley pleaded with James and the hostile.

Ava flipped her arm up, praying silently as she did so. *Please, God! Let me kill this man before he kills James.* Ava imagined the man's head directly behind her own, and a little to the left. She took a deep breath and held it tightly, closing her eyes and clenching her jaw as if she could will the bullet to find the center of the man's brain.

BANG!

The weight of the man with his arm around her neck pulled Ava to the floor.

Instantly, Foley rushed forward and kicked the pistol from the invader's hand. He lunged on top of the assailant and twisted his arm around to the back, while pushing Ava away from the fallen man in one singular, fluid motion.

James doubled over and vomited.

Ava watched as Foley restrained the man with the hole in his head. Her body shuddered at what she'd just been through. "I think he's dead."

# CHAPTER 5

The wealth of the sinner is laid up for the just.

Proverbs 13:22b

Ava held Buckley's leash tight. He barked frantically as Ulysses' new truck sped down the gravel drive to the house. "It's okay, Buck. Friends."

Ulysses and Sam Hodge both jumped out of the truck with weapons drawn. They ran up to the porch, pausing at the doorway.

Sam looked down at Charity who was mopping up blood from the hardwood floor. "What happened?"

"We got hit." Ava used all her strength to control Buckley who was still acting erratically.

"Where's Betty? Is she alright?" Sam stepped over the mess.

"A little shaken-up, but otherwise she's fine. She's lying down. None of us were injured," Ava said.

Sam hurried past Ava toward the master bedroom.

Ulysses calmly put his hand out for Buckley to sniff. "Everything is okay, fella." He looked Ava in her eyes. "Are you good?"

She nodded. "Yeah. They came out of nowhere."

"Hey, you guys made it back." Foley stood at the door. His hands were covered in blood from hauling out the dead bodies.

"Where did you put the dead?" Ulysses asked.

"Around back. James helped me get them out of the house. Betty was freaking out. I figured we'd ask Sam where he wants us to bury them."

"How many?"

"Six."

Without asking, Ulysses took control of the cleanup operation. "We'll throw them in the back of the box truck and take it to a public spot. We can set it on fire and save ourselves the trouble of digging a hole."

Foley tilted his head to the side. "That truck might come in handy for something."

Ulysses shook his head. "It might get us caught. If the rest of their people come looking for them, that truck will stick out like a sore thumb. We have to ditch it, and the Civic."

"What about the guns? We can keep those, right?" Foley seemed reluctant but fell in under

Ulysses' assumed command.

"Yeah. Guns, ammo, load-bearing equipment, and anything else they have of value. But the vehicles have got to go. We passed a concrete plant out on 71. We'll drive out there and burn them."

"Okay." Even battle-hardened Foley put a grim expression on his face at the harsh directive. Ava had only given Foley a brief synopsis of what her father used to do for a living.

Then, like a switch had been flipped, Ulysses took Ava's hand with all the gentleness of a tender father. "You had to kill one of them?"

She nodded.

"It's tough."

"I'm okay."

"You might be now, but this kind of thing has a way of sneaking up on you when everything is quiet. Remember, you did what you had to do."

"I know. And I'll be alright. I had to shoot someone before."

"Oh?"

"Antifa thugs tried to jump us after the Ross rally." She'd violated her pact of silence with Charity and James, but the vow had been made when she'd thought Austin PD was her worst problem. Things were different now.

Ulysses didn't interrogate her further. Rather, he gently put the back of his hand to her cheek. "Good girl," he whispered with a wink.

Ulysses walked to the door. "Charity, we'll help you get the rest of this cleaned up when we get back."

"Please be safe." She paused from her frenzied

scrubbing to glance outside toward James. "And take care of him. He . . . isn't like you and Foley."

"He's tougher than you think, but I'll look out for him." Ulysses waved at Ava as he left.

That evening, Ava did what she could to help an exhausted James and a weary Charity prepare dinner. Betty did not come out of her room all evening. Sam emerged from his room from time to time but spent most of the evening caring for his distraught wife. Ulysses set up the radios while Foley stood guard.

Ava ate her evening meal on the porch with Foley to keep him company. "I could pull the night shift with you if you want."

"I'd like that. James will have a tough time staying awake tonight after an all-nighter last night and that adrenaline dump today."

"What about you?"

"I'll be okay. He's not used to these conditions."

"It's been a while for you."

"You never forget." The corners of Foley's mouth turned down, as if he were forlorn. "It's like riding a bike."

Ulysses came out onto the porch. "Foley, here's a radio for you. I'll take your dishes inside if you'll hand them to me."

Ava passed her empty plate to Ulysses. "Thank you."

"You're welcome. Foley, I didn't sleep at all last night. I'm going to go to bed in the trailer. My walkie-talkie is on if you even think you see something. You should use the room over the garage as your observation post. It has the best view of the drive, which is the most likely avenue of approach for any hostiles."

"Yes, sir." Foley handed him his plate. "Ava volunteered to keep watch with me tonight since James may not be in the best condition."

Ulysses stared blankly at Foley. He said nothing for several seconds.

Foley stood up and added nervously, "If that's okay with you."

Ulysses broke his empty gaze and glanced at Ava then turned back to Foley. Finally, he ended his silence. "Sure. There's an extra rifle by the window."

Foley seemed not to breathe until Ulysses had gone back inside.

"What was all that about?" Ava let Foley help her up until she could get her balance on her crutches. "I just met the man. I don't need his permission for anything. And neither do you."

Foley waited until Ulysses was out of earshot. "He hasn't given me a lot of details about his old job, but he was obviously operating under much more lax rules of engagement than the regular military. Your dad . . . knows how to handle business. I'm guessing Tier 1 or private sector equivalent. Let's just say I respect him and don't want to do anything to get on his bad side."

"What happened when you guys took the vehicles to the concrete plant?" Ava followed Foley toward the garage.

"He had us park both of them together. He knifed the tires, cut strips out of the tires, pierced the fuel tanks, doused the strips with the fuel as it drained, then used the strips of the tires as wicks. He took one strip of tire dipped in fuel and placed it at the base of each tire.

"He didn't talk, didn't ask for help, and the entire operation took less than five minutes. By the time we were all in his truck and leaving the scene, both vehicles were engulfed in flames. This was something he'd done before.

"He'd obviously made a mental note of the concrete plant's location when he drove out to Marble Falls this morning. Very calculated."

Ava navigated her crutches through the side door of the garage which led up the stairs to the finished room over the garage, or FROG for short. "You're frightening me."

Foley waited patiently behind Ava, shining his flashlight so she could see to climb the stairs. "I'm just glad he's on our team."

Ava reached the top of the stairs and flipped on the lights.

"Turn that off. We have to maintain light and sound discipline."

Ava quickly flicked off the light switch. "Sorry."

"I should have told you. It's my fault." Foley directed the beam of his light around the room. "See what I mean?"

"What?" Ava followed the light as Foley directed it.

Foley put the beam on the bed which had been pulled up to within a few feet of the window. The curtains were open just enough for a person lying prone on the bed with a rifle to have a wide field of fire, but not be visually exposed to an outside threat. "He's got the FROG set up like a sniper's nest."

Foley handed the radio to Ava. "You're on comms." He positioned some pillows to support the barrel of his rifle, then lay down on the bed, looking out the window.

Ava put a pillow against the wall and lowered herself down onto the floor. "Let me know if you get sleepy. I can take over for you."

"I'll probably take you up on that offer in a couple hours. Why don't you see if you can get some rest in the meantime?"

"Okay." Ava had no intention of going to sleep, but in a matter of minutes, her eyes were closed and she was out.

The first light of daybreak illuminated the darkness which Ava had been monitoring through Foley's night vision scope for the past two hours. Her eyelids were heavy.

Someone knocked on the door downstairs.

"What was that!" Foley had been sleeping on the floor in the corner.

"Somebody knocking."

Foley jumped up. "Did you see anyone approach?" he whispered.

"No." Foley looked cautiously out the window to see who was below. "It's Betty."

Ava sat up on the bed. "She's probably not much of a threat."

Foley smirked. "I'll go downstairs and see what she wants."

Seconds later, Foley returned upstairs with Betty

behind him. She carried a thermos of coffee and two plates of French toast.

"Sam said he can take over if you two want to get some sleep after breakfast."

"Thank you. In that case, I better skip the coffee." Ava took the plate as Betty passed it to her.

"I figured you might want to take him up on the offer. I took the liberty of making you decaf."

"You thought of everything, Mrs. Hodge." Foley took the thermos.

"It's the least I can do. I'm afraid I'm not cut out for the rough-and-tumble stuff. So, I'll try to make myself useful in the garden and in the kitchen."

"How are you holding up this morning?" Ava asked.

"Better." She nodded decisively. "Sam keeps a close eye on potential threats." Betty looked at Ava. "You know how he is; always keeping up with what might happen in the markets, cyber threats, that sort of thing. So, we're fairly well prepared, at least from a provisions standpoint. But, you know, it's always been one close call or another. First, it was Y2K, then it was solar storms, then it was a currency collapse; seems we're always getting ready for something. He's been watching this social unrest thing for a while, too. I've always gone along with whatever he recommends—even took charge of the gardening and canning."

Betty looked out the window as warm hues of orange daylight slowly crept in. "Since Sam took care of everything, I always figured that if anything ever happened, we'd be just fine. I never even got worried when Austin started having trouble. Then, yesterday, when I heard the gunshots, and when I walked in the house and saw all that blood; in my house, where I thought I was so safe. I don't know; I guess it just turned my world upside down.

"Sam would always talk about other people who weren't getting prepared because of what he called *normalcy bias*. He says they don't think anything bad can happen to them because nothing bad has ever happened to them before. I never thought I could fall victim to that. After all, we were getting ready for every threat imaginable. Moving to the country, storing food, raising chickens, growing a garden, fruit trees."

She shook her head. "But I suppose I had my own version of normalcy bias. Because I never thought I'd see something like that in my own living room. I'm sorry I melted down like that. I think I'll be more mentally prepared for it if it happens again."

Ava took Betty's hand and pulled it to her chest. "It's good to be ready for it; mentally, physically, and spiritually, but we'll pray it doesn't happen again."

Betty nodded. "Thank you. I'm sure glad you all were here. Things would have turned out very differently if it had only been me and Sam."

# CHAPTER 6

Whoso findeth a wife findeth a good thing, and obtaineth favour of the Lord.

Proverbs 18:22

Three weeks passed after the election. President Ross augmented the National Guard with troops from the regular army to restore order in the largest cities across America. No other attacks came against Sam Hodge's property, but like most major metropolitan areas, Austin remained dangerous and barely livable.

Ava walked into the living room to find Charity sitting on the couch Wednesday morning. "The electricity is back on! That's great! Is the news saying what caused the outage?"

"They say the government shut down the grid

and the internet to stifle anti-Ross protestors. But that doesn't make any sense. Ross wouldn't do that. I think the opposition did it so they could blame it on Ross."

Ava took a seat beside her.

Charity looked at her foot. "How's the ankle?"

"Feels great." Ava moved her foot in a circular motion.

Charity pressed her lips together. "You should at least keep it wrapped up."

"Yeah, I'll put an Ace bandage on it after breakfast. I didn't hear you come to bed last night. Did you stay up to keep watch with James?"

Charity held her hand over her face and wouldn't look Ava in the eye. "Something like that."

"Oh." Ava dropped the subject.

"Anyway, we're going to drive down to Buda today. Things seem to be fairly calm with the military enforcing curfew and all."

"The military is only in Austin. You'll be driving through forty miles of backroads to get to Buda. What are you going down there for?"

"We just need Pastor Greg to perform a quick ceremony for us. We'll get it all formalized at the courthouse after things get back to normal. But it's obvious we're not going to get to have the wedding we were hoping for in December. Plus, now that we're living under the same roof, we need to go ahead and make our vows before God."

"I see." Ava listened to the news for a while then asked, "Do you even know that Pastor Greg will be there? With the curfew, I doubt he's been holding Wednesday night service."

"We have to try." Charity looked at Ava with desperate eyes. "We *need* to get married as soon as possible."

"Are you pregnant?"

"No!" Charity looked offended.

"Sorry."

Charity lost her indignant tone. "At least if I am, it would be way too early to know."

"Ooooh." The puzzle pieces fell neatly into place within Ava's mind. She was quiet for another moment. "Why don't you let Foley perform the service? We could have the wedding right here!"

"Foley?"

"Sure, he led the Bible study at Faith House for several months. He took over Pastor Jon's position after he was promoted at Faith Chapel. Why not?"

Charity grunted and put her head in her hand. "I don't want everyone knowing my business. I feel so ashamed."

Ava put her arm around her friend. "The only person you owe an apology to is God. Tell him you're sorry, make things right, and move on. Don't worry about what the people in this house think. Do you think if the two of you run off for the day, then come back and start sleeping in the same room, people here aren't going to know what's going on?"

Charity looked up. "You're right. Do you think we can put it together today?"

"Plan a wedding? In one day? Charity, the damage is already done. If we have it today or next week, what's the difference?"

Charity sighed. "Then there's tonight, and tomorrow night, and the night after. It's one thing to abstain, and it's quite another to stop something you've started."

Ava huffed. "I wouldn't know."

"Yeah, well, keep it that way. Trust me, you need to cut out those overnight watch shifts with Foley while you still can. Or better yet, make it a double wedding!"

Ava shook her head. "I like him, but I'm not ready for all of that."

"Then put the kibosh on those watch shifts together."

"We just take turns keeping watch. We don't even kiss when we're on duty."

"That's how it starts. But do you think you can keep it like that if we're still in this situation three months from now?"

"The new election is next Tuesday. We'll know something then and be able to put together a plan for the future."

"Ava, I'm just saying. You know how much James and I wanted to honor God. If you don't put the proper barriers up, you're failing to plan and planning to fail."

She considered her friend's advice. It was true. Charity and James were the most dedicated Christians she knew. If they couldn't make it, then perhaps she was being a little naive to think she and Foley were above being tempted into sin. "I'll talk to Betty about having a small wedding and reception."

"Try to convince her that it needs to be today. Nothing special. Don't go out of your way and don't let Betty make a fuss over it."

"I'll do what I can." Ava gave her friend a hug.

"Without giving her all the sordid details." Charity looked at Ava with puppy dog eyes.

"Our secret." Ava smiled.

That afternoon, Foley wore his best polo shirt and his nicest cargo pants as he stood by the river with his Bible in hand. Like most everyone else, he had not brought any dress clothes to the Hodges' property. Still, he looked dashing to Ava as she followed her friend between the chairs. Sam and Betty Hodge sat on one side, with Ulysses and Buckley on the other. Ulysses kept his battle rifle low and mostly out of sight, as if he were making a diligent effort not ruin the atmosphere, but everyone knew if they were to get any Antifa wedding crashers, the weapon would be a welcomed object.

James stood next to Foley. Sam had offered him a jacket, but it was much too wide and much too short for James. Nevertheless, the groom appeared quite presentable in a pair of dark jeans and a button-down white shirt.

Charity had the foresight to bring a dress with her when they came out to Sam's place. Being very late in the fall, the dress was navy blue rather than white. Ava figured that most likely spared her friend some level of self-imposed guilt and internal conflict. Perhaps it was for the best.

Flower selections were sparse, but Ava was able to locate a few wild plants with some color from around the property. They were long green stems with fluffy purple rods at the top. Betty had referred to them as Violet Blazing Stars, but Ava wasn't sure. A navy-blue ribbon which Betty had scrounged up was tied ornamentally around the stems of the flowers.

Charity looked pretty. James looked happy. Ava knew the two were deeply in love and would make a wonderful couple, committed to each other, and even though they'd slipped up, they were committed to honoring God.

Once Charity and Ava arrived at the river's edge, Foley opened his Bible. "And He answered and said unto them, 'Have ye not read, that He which made them at the beginning made them male and female.' And said, 'For this cause shall a man leave father and mother, and shall cleave to his wife: and they twain shall be one flesh? Wherefore they are no more twain, but one flesh. What therefore God hath joined together, let not man put asunder.'"

Charity and James each read their own vows which they'd written to each other. Then Foley prayed for God to bless and protect their marriage. Afterward, he looked up. "I now pronounce you husband and wife."

James kissed Charity passionately while the others clapped.

Betty announced. "I've put together some refreshments on the back deck. I'd have done more if I had known, but it seems time was of the essence for this particular ceremony." She paused, putting her finger to her lip. "Oh dear! In all the hurry I've forgotten to ice the cake!"

# CHAPTER 7

Then Peter and the other apostles answered and said, We ought to obey God rather than men.

Acts 5:29

Wednesday evening after the wedding, Ava sat on the loveseat with Foley watching the news. Sam and Betty sat on the couch. Ulysses was in the room above the garage keeping watch. James and Charity were . . . nowhere to be found. *Breaking News* scrolled across the bottom of the screen.

"It should say *Propaganda Alert*. I wonder what load of bovine excrement they're about to hand us now?" Ava crossed her arms tightly in anticipation of the media network's heavily tilted view of the news.

The female anchor wore next to no makeup and a high-and-tight haircut, which lent her the impression of a drill sergeant. She spoke with a low voice, which also would not have been out of place for someone instructing a military boot camp.

"The House and Senate have ended a closed-door session on Capitol Hill. The rare joint session was convened in secrecy early today and the details of the meeting are coming to you in real time as they are released to us.

"The clandestine assembly appears to have been a streamlined impeachment process to remove President Ross who has been taken into custody by the US Marshals Service for obstruction of justice, abuse of power, usurping the Constitution, and inciting a riot. Congress has determined that Ross' actions to overturn the election results in Florida and Texas not only violated the sacred trust of the American people, but also led to the wide-spread riots which destroyed parts of DC, New York, Atlanta, Chicago, LA, and so many other cities around the nation.

"The unprecedented speed at which these hearings were conducted and completed represented an effort to circumvent next week's election do-over in Texas and Florida."

"They've just shot themselves in the foot!" Ava motioned to the television screen with her open hand. "Blackwell will take office, and he'll cause the liberals ten times the trouble Ross would have. I've got to go tell my dad!"

Foley held her arm to restrain her from getting up. "Wait for it."

The reporter continued. "Congress has appointed Speaker of the House Steve Woods to serve as the interim POTUS until next month's inauguration. The special impeachment committee made up of top leadership from both houses determined that Michael Ross' VP selection naming Idaho Governor Turner Blackwell as successor to the oval office is not binding due to the felonious actions against the state. No criminal action is being taken against the Idaho governor at this time."

"Unbelievable!" Ava stood up and headed for the door.

"Take it easy on those stairs," Sam warned. "Put your weight on the handrails. If you get overly rambunctious, you'll be back on those crutches for another two weeks."

"And bring your rifle," Foley added. "We can't get in the habit of breaking protocol."

Ava stopped in her tracks, turned to go back to her room, retrieved her AR-15, then rushed off to tell her father the troublesome news. She considered Sam's caveat but sprinted up the stairs regardless.

"Is everything okay?" Ulysses stood at the top of the stairs.

"Yes and no." She placed her rifle by the door, flopped down on the bed and proceeded to relay the information from the news broadcast.

"Well, that's not good." Ulysses turned back toward the window. "I'm sure they'll fast-track

Markovich's gun ban . . . for the good of the country."

"What do we do?" Ava folded her hands.

"Can you keep an eye out for raiders? I'm going to grab my laptop from the trailer."

"Sure."

"Use my gun. It's got a better sight." Ulysses handed Ava his rifle and took hers as he hurried down the stairs.

Ava watched the driveway through her father's night vision sight. She could see every detail, just as if she were looking out the window in broad daylight. "Whoa! This is way better than Foley's night vision sight. I guess these things are not all created equal."

Minutes later, Ulysses returned and opened his laptop.

"What are you looking for?" she asked.

"I'm checking the conservative underground threads."

"Oh, so our team is on the dark web, too?"

"Sort of. When Twitter, YouTube, and Facebook started deleting accounts and shadow banning right-leaning users, many of them went straight underground. Everyone knew it was only a matter of time until the political pendulum swung back to the far left. If Markovich doesn't completely take down the internet, I'm sure a lot of patriots will start finding out about the conservative darknet."

Ulysses typed in a URL into the address bar. "I found a couple message boards that conservatives in the military are using. Some speculation had already started that Markovich might try something like this. These guys aren't planning to fall in line."

"Markovich didn't do it. It was Congress."

"Markovich is pulling the strings. Woods is just a puppet. So is Congress, for that matter." Ulysses pecked away at the keyboard.

Ava moved her eyes back and forth from watching the scope to looking at what her father was doing. "Are you finding anything out?"

"Yep. It seems Blackwell and Ross' Cabinet got wind of what was going on. The remaining members of the Liberty Caucus sent encrypted text messages via Wire to let them know what was happening."

"And?"

Ulysses kept reading. "It looks like Secretary of Defense Albert Domingo started moving US military troops and assets to conservative states who are planning to secede."

"Wow! There really is going to be a civil war!" Ava looked up from the scope. "But why is the head of the DOD sending troops and equipment to the seceding states? They'll be prepositioned to take down the resistance."

Ulysses shook his head. "He's giving the equipment to the states."

"How can he do that?"

"The 1033 Program. It's been on the books for years. DOD is fully in charge of it."

"I thought that was only for surplus equipment."

"Yep. And Secretary of Defense Domingo decides what qualifies as surplus material."

"Woods and Markovich will just reverse the order."

Ulysses nodded. "I'm sure they will, but much of the equipment will already be relocated by the time they find out what's happened. And by then, it will be an act of war for the US military to set foot on the sovereign soil of the independent states."

"What about the troops? How do the governors of the conservative states know they'll side with them?"

"They don't. But being in the state, under the orders of the secretary of defense, to follow the command of those governors will help nudge the troops in the right direction."

"Don't you think most of the military will side with Ross and Blackwell in this thing? They've taken an oath to the Constitution. Markovich is obviously running roughshod over it with his gun ban. I'm sure they'll stand up for the Second Amendment."

Ulysses looked at her. "You mean like the cops who stood up for the Second Amendment when Ray Nagin ordered all the guns to be confiscated in New Orleans in the wake of Katrina?"

Ava looked up from the rifle again. She thought for a while. "I guess I don't remember those cops."

"Yeah, because they didn't exist. You've heard of the Milgram experiment, right?"

"Sounds familiar. Remind me."

"Milgram was a psychologist who ran an experiment back in the 60s. He was examining the claims of the war criminals tried in the Nuremberg trials who said they were only following orders.

"Milgram paid random people four dollars and fifty cents to participate. He'd put the subject at a desk to read paired words which another person would have to remember. The person who had to remember the word pairs was actually an actor, but the subject didn't know that. Each time the actor got a wrong answer, the subject was instructed to give the actor an electric shock. With each subsequent wrong answer, the subject had to administer an increasingly higher level of shock, or so he thought.

"With only the professor as an authority figure telling them to continue the experiment, two-thirds of the subjects administered all the way up to what they believed to be a lethal level of electric shock.

"Nothing was on the line but a measly four dollars and fifty cents."

"Yes!" Ava turned. "They recreated that experiment about a decade ago, paying the participants fifty bucks. Seems like the outcome was about the same. About two-thirds of the people gave the highest level of shock."

Ulysses lowered his head. "So that's random people doing it for fifty dollars. Imagine a group of people who have been trained to believe that chain of command is everything. The numbers will be much higher."

Ava looked through the scope. "Foley belongs to a group called Oath Keepers. It's former and active military and law enforcement who have reaffirmed their oath to the Constitution. They've specifically vowed not to engage in anti-Constitutional activities like disarming the public, warrantless searches, and detaining Americans as enemy combatants. They won't go along with Markovich."

Ulysses nodded. "People who have already made

up their minds about what they're going to do when the stuff hits the fan, they'll be on the right side. But they're in the minority."

"Does it say which states are getting the equipment?"

Ulysses shook his head. "No, but I'm sure Idaho is on the list."

"What about Texas?"

"Not even close. The reason Antifa chose this state to go after to swing the election was because it was already teetering on the verge of going liberal. The influx of Democrats from California, years of unenforced immigration law, combined with Texas' institutes of higher learning made it an easy election to steal.

"Oklahoma is on the top-ten list for reddest states. That's where my homestead is. It's not as fancy as the doctor's here, but I've got all the resources we need to ride this thing out. You should talk to your friends and ask them to go there. We'll make room for everybody."

Ava sat up on the bed. "Leave Texas?"

"You don't have anything to leave. Your apartment has been burned. Sam won't be able to reopen his office until all this is sorted out, so you don't have a job. These people are all you have, and we can take them with us. What's more, they'll all be safe. You don't want to stay here, Ava. Texas is going to be a war zone. I've spent too much of my life living in a war zone. So has Foley. It changed us both—for the worse. And if you stay here, even if you live through it, you won't be the same. I'm begging you, please; come back to Oklahoma with me."

Ava's mouth hung open in shock. "I . . . I don't know what to say."

"Just say you'll think about it; that you'll talk it over with the group."

She shook her head slowly. "And give up? Texas is my home. I don't want to let Markovich and the communists have it without a fight."

"Ava, this is not your fight. I'm sure Oklahoma is one of the states that will secede. We can support the effort from there."

"I don't want to go to Oklahoma and fight. I want to fight here."

"No, you're not understanding me. We can support them without fighting. I've got a huge farm. We can grow crops and support the war effort with resources."

"What? Be farmers? If every conservative decides to farm instead of fight, then Markovich won't have much trouble at all. In fact, he'll likely be very well-fed; and have a very well-fed army!"

Ava stood up from the bed. Her face was glowing a bright hue of vermilion. "I don't blame Antifa for any of this. They're just doing what they believe in—what they've been programmed to think. In fact, I respect them. At least when they have a core conviction, they take action."

Ava put her hands on her hips and leaned forward toward her father. "Do you know who I blame for this mess? Armchair conservatives who won't do anything except sit around and watch Fox News all day and complain about how the liberals are stealing their country. Well, I've got news for you; the liberals didn't steal anything. The conservatives abandoned their post; like walking away from a car on the freeway. The liberals happen to be walking by, saw a fine-looking vehicle on the side of the road, gassed up, keys in the ignition. Who can blame them? From their perspective, it probably looked like no one wanted it, so why not put it to good use?"

She shook her head violently. "And Antifa, those poor kids went to the schools your generation sent them to; schools that conservatives allowed to be hijacked by the communists. Schools that taught them there is no God. The Antifa kids watched the propaganda movies put out by Hollywood that their mothers and fathers paid for them to watch; no one ever told them any different. Conservative complacency, that's why this is all happening. It's not even fair to blame these poor mindless zombies who don't know their brains from a blob of warm lard.

"If you want conservatives to do anything, you have to tie it to a tax bill. They'll stand idly by while children are murdered, atheism is taught in schools and the country is taken over by communists, but tell them they'll get an extra hundred bucks back from the IRS and they'll move heaven and earth."

She glared at him. "Now you want to go be a farmer." Ava looked away with tight fists and a tight jaw.

"Ava, every day for the past thirty years, I've wished I hadn't taken that job; wished I'd been there for my child. If I could have changed that one thing, I'd have been a good father. I'd have fought against the school system. I'd have been involved in politics. I'd have protested, whatever I could have done to make this a better country for you.

"The paychecks were phenomenal, especially for the nineties. But that's not why I did what I did. I was fighting communism; trying to make this a better world for everybody. At least that's what I thought."

Guilt washed through Ava's soul like a flood of septic shame. She lowered her head, appalled at what she'd just said to this poor man who'd endured so much and been abandoned for decades by his country. Why should he want to fight? He'd given his all and received nothing in return.

Tears of self-condemnation formed at the corners of her eyes. She wiped her face with the sleeve of her shirt. She took a deep breath and sat on the bed next to her father. "I'm sorry. You didn't deserve that. I wish I could take back everything I just said to you."

She took his hand. "Please forgive me."

"Hey, it's okay." He pulled her head close to his.

The two of them sat on the bed for several minutes without speaking.

Ava interrupted the quietness. "You don't owe this country anything. They used you and tossed you out like a sour dish rag. But Texas is my home. And I have to take a stand. Go back to Oklahoma. When it's all over, I'll come get you, and we'll live out our days together, right here in Texas."

Ulysses pulled back from her, holding her head in his hands. He bit his lip as tears ran down his chin. "Ava, I'm never leaving you again. If you're determined to fight, I'll be right by your side."

# CHAPTER 8

For ye know what commandments we gave
you by the Lord Jesus. For this is the will of
God, even your sanctification, that ye should
abstain from fornication: That every one of
you should know how to possess his vessel
in sanctification and honour; Not in the lust
of concupiscence, even as the Gentiles
which know not God.

1 Thessalonians 4:2-5

Ava leaned over and put her hand on Foley's
back as he lay on the bed with his eye against the
night vision scope. "So that's where we're at. I'm
sort of assuming you're on the same page as me and
my dad, I just don't know about everyone else."

"I'm in."

She smiled and lowered herself on his wide back. "Thanks. I'm worried that my dad might not be up for it."

"Why?"

"Everything he's been through. He's dealing with some serious PTSD."

"From what I've seen, and from what you told me about how he handled those guys at the polling station, I don't think his PTSD is likely to affect his ability to function in a combat situation. I've been through it myself and I've seen it in plenty of other guys. Your dad's problem is most likely sleeping, nightmares; you see those thousand-yard stares he gets from time to time. It's not healthy but your dad probably feels more comfortable in a firefight than going out to eat at a restaurant."

"What do you think the others will say?" She ran her fingers up and down his back, feeling the muscles.

"You know them better than me." Foley let the rifle fall sideways on the bed and turned over to kiss Ava. He gripped her shoulders, then let his hands run down her torso to her waist. He kissed her passionately and she melted into his arms.

Minutes later, Foley stood up from the bed. "We can't do this. My pulse is pounding like a drum." He shook his head. "Besides the slippery slope we're getting on morally, I'm supposed to be watching the drive. I'm sorry, Ava. We can't work watch shifts together. I simply don't have the willpower to control myself when I'm around you."

She took a deep breath and slowly let it back out.

"Yeah, I'm having the same problem. And don't apologize. I'm the one who started it. I'm sorry." Ava sat up on the bed and straightened her shirt. "But I'm going to miss hanging out with you up here."

Foley sat back down. "Me, too."

Ava took his hand. "While we're on the subject, I'm sure you've heard that James and Charity took the big room downstairs. That means I'll be moving upstairs, across the hall from you. We should go ahead and say visiting each other in our bedrooms is off limits." She bit her lip and looked him in the eyes. "Otherwise, it could be a little too convenient."

Foley nodded. "God told Cain to be careful because sin was crouching at his door. In our case, I guess it'll be right across the hall."

She giggled and gave him a quick peck on the lips.

Foley watched her for a few seconds.

Ava flipped her hair behind her ear. "What?"

He held her hand firmly. "We've only known each other for about three months. But being around you all the time, it's been . . . immersive."

"What the heck is that supposed to mean?"

He put his hand around her back. "It means . . ." He paused. "It means I'm falling in love with you."

Her cheeks warmed, her inside fluttered, and she gave up fighting the growing smile that threatened to go from one ear to the other. Ava let him pull her in for one more long, passionate kiss. She ran her fingers through his soft beard, then pushed him back. She gasped for air. "I better go while I still can."

Thursday evening, everyone was at the table for dinner except Ulysses who was on watch duty. After most of them had finished eating, Ava said, "I have an announcement to make before everyone gets up from the table."

Charity squealed. "You and Foley are getting married!"

Ava gritted her teeth and looked up. "No, Charity. We're not getting married, but thanks for embarrassing us."

"For now," Foley added.

"What?" Ava asked.

"We're not getting married for now."

Ava blushed, put her head on her hand and looked at the silverware on the table.

Foley attempted to clarify his statement. "We're not getting married for now, we don't have any plans to get married in the immediate future; I'm just saying that it's not something we've categorically ruled out."

Ava looked up at Foley who'd managed to embarrass himself. "Thank you for the more than adequate explanation. Now, back to what I was saying."

Ava relayed her stance on the apparent civil conflict brewing. She described her views, noting that Foley was on the same page as herself. She detailed the conversation she'd had with her father, and communicated the fact that while they did not see eye-to-eye on the matter, he would be taking a stand beside her in the confrontation. "I can't sit back and let the theft of my country go unchallenged. We're going to strike back. We'll launch an insurgency campaign against the regime. We'll blow stuff up, attack critical infrastructure, whatever we can to harass the enemy.

"Sam, you and Betty have been more than generous letting us stay here. I can't ask you to turn a blind eye to our activities, so if you have the least bit of reservation, let me know and we'll move on. We'll take every precaution not to lead them back here, but if we're found out, it could place you both in grave danger.

"James, you and Charity have to make your own decision. If it's not something you want to be involved with, we'll appreciate your support through prayer."

Betty held her napkin over her mouth. Ava could only imagine the gaping view of Mrs. Hodge's tonsils had it not been for the modesty offered by the thin serviette. Betty's eyes showed her astonishment over the subject matter as they shifted to her husband. While not nearly as perplexed as his wife, Sam also seemed to be at a loss for words and particularly unsure how to address Betty's bewilderment.

James and Charity gazed upon each other with a sense of fortitude. This, Ava did not expect. But even with the foreshadowing of the couple's expression, Ava was amazed when James spoke.

His reply echoed the inner determination and certainty Ava had seen in his eyes. "Charity and I are with you."

Charity glanced proudly at her husband, then

turned to Ava and Foley. She nodded briskly in concurrence.

Betty's eyes batted repeatedly with hesitation and fear. "We'll have to talk this over, Ava. I'm just not sure we're willing to put everything on the line."

Sam's expression lacked grit. He added nothing to what his wife had said but seemed all too satisfied with her response.

Ava said, "Like I said, I completely understand. Take all the time you need. If you need us to go, just say the word, and we'll be out in twenty-four hours. And I assure you we won't take any action toward preparing for war until we've left. The last thing I want to do is jeopardize the two of you or your property."

"I appreciate that." Sam's shoulders slumped and he swallowed hard. "If you'll all excuse me, I'm next on watch." He stood up and left the table without looking any of them in the eye.

Ava and Foley cleaned up the dishes after supper.

"I've got next watch. I'm going to try to get some sleep before my shift." Foley kissed Ava on the forehead.

"Okay, see you later." She hung the dish towel on the handle of the stove to dry.

Ulysses walked into the kitchen and made himself a plate from the leftovers. "Do you want to take the fishing poles back to the river?"

"It's pitch dark."

He sat at the counter and began eating. "Best

time to catch fish. We've got flashlights."

Ava wasn't sure about it being the optimum opportunity to reel in a big one, but she liked the idea of being alone with her father. "Okay. Let me grab my boots."

After Ulysses finished eating, the two of them walked the short distance to the river where Sam had a bench set up for just such an activity. Ulysses used his headlamp to see while he affixed an artificial lure to Ava's line. "You're all set."

"Great. What do I do?"

"You've never cast a line before?"

"The guy who was supposed to fill in for you wasn't much of a father."

"Right." Ulysses took Ava's pole. "Click the release then put your thumb on the line while you cock the lure back over your shoulder. Give it a good whip forward and take your thumb off the line." Ulysses demonstrated. The lure dropped in the water several yards out. "Then give it a quick turn, and the line will lock."

"Can I try?"

"Sure. Hold this one while I set up the other pole."

Once Ulysses had the lure attached to the second pole, he exchanged it for the rod Ava was holding.

"Here it goes." Ava attempted to replicate Ulysses' cast. ZZZzzzzzzz. Plop! It didn't go nearly as far as Ulysses' cast, but she felt proud of the effort. She turned the handle on the reel but it immediately began spinning. "I did something wrong. What is it doing?"

"You've got a fish! Give it a good firm tug to set

the hook."

Ava jerked the pole up. "Like that?"

Ulysses bobbed his head from side to side. "If he's still on there, then it'll work."

"Now what?"

"Reel him in. Nice and smooth."

Ava did so.

Ulysses walked to the bank. He reached down and pulled the fish from the water. "Striped bass. These are good eatin'." The scales of the two-foot-long fish glistened in the beam of Ulysses' headlamp.

"I caught a fish! I had no idea it was this easy!"

"It's usually not," Ulysses confirmed. "I wouldn't expect that to happen too often if I were you." Ulysses removed the lure from the fish's jaw and placed the bass in the bucket which he'd filled with water from the river.

Ava recast her line and waited anxiously for the next fish. She reeled in the line, recast, then repeated the procedure over and over for the next fifteen minutes. Her casting improved, but no other fish seemed interested.

"How did your dinner conversation go?"

Ava sighed. "James and Charity are in; which surprised me. Sam and Betty seem a little freaked out by the whole thing; which didn't surprise me."

"Do you have any ideas on where to go if the Hodges don't want to get involved?"

"No." She reeled in her line with a slow, mechanical motion, betraying her thoughts which were miles away from the river and the fish therein. "I'll ask Foley tomorrow. He must have some guys he used to shoot with. Maybe one of them will have some land where we can camp out in the trailer."

Ulysses sent his lure flinging end over end toward the other side of the Pedernales River. "We can link up with some other like-minded people if need be. But that will likely mean that we'll be under someone else's command, who may or may not be qualified to lead." His headlamp flashed in her direction, then back to the red-and-white bobber in the water. "We currently have five people. We can launch a fairly effective insurgency campaign with that many. Small is good. Small is harder to detect, easy to move around, and has a limited verbal footprint."

"Limited verbal footprint?"

"Yeah, the fewer people you have on a team, the lower the odds are that somebody will say something to someone they shouldn't."

"Oh. Loose lips sink ships."

"Exactly."

Ava and her father spent two more hours at the bank of the river. Ava caught two more fish. Ulysses caught one. The catch would be sufficient for everyone to have a taste the next day for lunch.

Early Friday morning, Ava sat on the stairs of the front porch with Foley and Buckley. Buckley put his head in her lap. She scratched his ears. "You've been doing a great job out here by yourself, Buck. I know it seems like a thankless job, but we all appreciate it. You hear stuff we can't."

Ava took another biscuit from the pocket of her hoodie and fed it to her pet. His mouth smacked like a pair of galoshes mucking through puddles of mud.

Foley looked up from his phone to see why the dog was making such a racket. "Are you smuggling him bacon in those biscuits?"

"He's the hardest working member of this team. He deserves it." Ava held her hand out for Buckley to lick.

Foley turned his attention back to his phone. "I can't think of anywhere that would be safe to go. Everyone I know lives in town. Most of them have left, gone somewhere else to stay with friends or family."

"Could we all stay at your old place if my dad kept his trailer in your drive? Your neighborhood isn't as densely populated as most areas around Austin."

"Lost Creek isn't that far from downtown." Foley shook his head. "I wouldn't feel comfortable there."

"What about the National Forest north of Houston?"

"We'd have nowhere to keep supplies, and all five of us would be in that little travel trailer. It would be really tight. If we have to leave, I think you should consider taking your dad up on his offer to go out to his place."

"No way!" Ava dried off the dog slobber from her hands onto her jeans.

Foley held up a hand. "Hear me out. I'm not suggesting that we avoid the fight, but we could use his place as a forward operating base. We could amass supplies, plan raids into enemy territory, all under the protection of Oklahoma, which has declared themselves to be a sovereign state."

"His place is in the north-east corner of Oklahoma. It's not exactly a short hike across the border to get back in the fight. Dallas is the closest major Texas city and that's probably 300 miles from his place, from what he's told me."

"We've got the trailer. We can use it for a fallback position when we go on missions."

"Oklahoma and Texas are both going to be guarding the border."

"That's a lot of border to hold down. The Red River border is every bit of 300 miles long; maybe 350."

"Like you said, it's a river." Ava scratched Buckley's belly. "We're not going to drive a travel trailer across it without a bridge, and I guarantee both sides will have people on the bridges."

"You might not drive a travel trailer across it, but you can take a four-wheeler with a snorkel over it. Unless it's been raining, Red River is seldom more than three feet deep."

Ava let her head sink into her hand as she considered the predicament. "Dad said he'd find another team for us to link up with if need be."

Foley huffed. "I know. But neither your father nor I like that idea. It's a big gamble to join up with some random group of hotheads who may or may not know what they're doing."

Sam came out the front door. "Ava, can you and Foley come into the kitchen? Betty and I want to talk to you."

"Sure. We'll be right there." She raised her eyebrows at Foley. "This is the big moment. If they

say we have to go, we've got 'til this time tomorrow
to figure it out."

# CHAPTER 9

Two are better than one; because they have a good reward for their labour. For if they fall, the one will lift up his fellow: but woe to him that is alone when he falleth; for he hath not another to help him up. Again, if two lie together, then they have heat: but how can one be warm alone? And if one prevail against him, two shall withstand him; and a threefold cord is not quickly broken.

Ecclesiastes 4:9-12

Ava took a seat at the counter. Foley stood behind her stool. Ava asked, "What did you decide?"

Sam looked at his wife. "We didn't sleep last

night. Betty and I were up discussing what you said. A large part of our conversation focused on the hope that the worst won't happen but watching the news this morning, I'm afraid that's just wishful thinking.

"Wyoming, Nebraska, and Kansas have announced that they're joining Idaho, Montana, Oklahoma, and Utah in seceding from the Union. The Dakotas are both expected to make an official statement before the day's end, but the pundits seem to think the decision has already been made.

"Texas is the obvious missing link which keeps the Alliance of Independent States from forming a continuous border from Canada to Mexico. It will certainly be a battleground state.

"We admire your conviction, Ava."

"But," she said.

Sam shook his head. "No but. If Texas can't be wrestled from the clutches of Markovich and his communist designs, we've already lost our home.

"We're further along in years than the rest of you and wouldn't be much assistance in combat roles, but we'll do what we can to help out. Our home is your home. We trust you'll keep your word; that you'll take precautions to avoid bringing unnecessary attention to our little farm, but we understand the risks."

Ava stood up from the stool and walked around the counter. She embraced Sam and held him tight for several seconds. When she finally let go, she hugged Betty as well. "Thank you. Thank you, both."

"No, Ava." Betty patted her on the back. "Thank

you for helping us to see what needs doing. We'd have never forgiven ourselves if we'd stuck our heads in the sand and pretended none of this was happening."

Sam smiled. "That would have been a short-lived strategy anyway, I'm sure."

"I'll let James and Charity know," Foley smiled and walked away.

Ava gripped Sam's hand. "Thanks again. I need to go tell my dad."

Saturday after breakfast, Ava worked with Charity to relocate soil from the compost bins to the raised bed garden. Buckley tagged along. Betty maintained three separate bins for various stages of decomposition. All three were simple constructions of salvaged wooden pallets.

Charity pushed the wheelbarrow up to the first bin. "Look. Something has been in the compost. It knocked over the pallet." Charity playfully patted Buckley on the side. "Buck, you're supposed to be on watch 24/7. How did you let this happen?"

"Maybe he's on strike. We haven't exactly been compensating him for overtime." Ava jabbed her shovel in the compost of the open bin. "Feral hogs. Those fish guts we put in there probably attracted them." Once her probe was finished, Ava replaced the front and top pallets, which had been knocked away.

Charity removed the dingy wooden pallet acting as a gate for the bin of the most decomposed material. "If a hog can move that pallet, you don't think one can get through the fence around the garden area?"

Using the shovel, Ava began filling the wheelbarrow with rich, dark compost. "A pig could probably root under, but I think Betty has her fence buried a couple inches below the surface. It would take a very determined hog to breach that."

Seemingly resigned to the fact that his professional guard-dog services were not required for the task of hauling dirt from one location to the other, Buckley sauntered over to the tree where he had a good view of Ava, the rabbit hutch, the chickens, and the house. He lay down in the grass, putting his head on one paw and slapping his tail sporadically against the ground.

Once the wheelbarrow was filled, Charity lifted the handles and pushed the dirt toward the garden bed where it was needed. "Betty was talking about expanding her operation so we'd have excess food to store or barter. If she does, she'll need more fence."

Ava followed her through the gate, then transferred the soil from the wheelbarrow to the raised bed garden. "Fencing material shouldn't be too hard to find. Staple foods, on the other hand, will be in short supply if supply chains become further disrupted because of the conflict."

"Sam stocked up a lot of staples. Plus, we all brought what we had." Charity backed the wheelbarrow out of the gate.

Ava trailed behind for another load. "Sam stocked up for two people. The rest of us probably brought less than an extra three months' worth of food, all total."

"Plus, the rabbits, chickens, and garden. That will go a long way. We don't even know that there will be a fight. Maybe the two sides will just let each other be. But even if we do have a war, I can't imagine it will last more than a few months."

Ava sighed as she chucked the tip of the shovel into the black compost. "That's what they thought at the beginning of the last civil war. This one could last just as long as the last one; even longer."

"I hope you're wrong about that." Charity moved the haul to the garden.

"Me, too. But I'm going to talk to the guys about making a run out to Marble Falls. I think we should pick up some more rice, coffee, flour, salt; that kind of stuff."

"We've got tactical training after lunch," Charity said.

"I know. Maybe tomorrow morning then." Ava paused to look at her friend. "How do you feel about that?"

"About what?"

"Tactical training."

Charity shook her head. "I know where you're going with this. I've already had this conversation with James. He signed off, so I'm good. But I appreciate your concern."

"Okay." Ava continued her task of spreading the compost evenly around the raised bed. The two girls continued working together quietly for several more minutes.

Charity dropped the handles of the wheelbarrow and put her hands on her hips. "Go ahead. Get it out of your system."

Ava huffed. "What? I didn't say anything."

"No, but you're thinking it. And that's worse. I've known you for a long time, Ava. I know when you've got something on your mind."

Ava didn't speak.

Charity stood adamantly. "It's the bridge. You're worried that I'm going to freak out and freeze up like I did on the bridge. You think I shouldn't be part of the fire team."

Ava spun the shovel nervously in her hands. "What do you think?"

"Honestly, I'm not sure. I told James that I would be fine and that I could handle myself, but I don't know." Charity walked the wheelbarrow toward the storage shed.

Ava walked behind her and exchanged the shovel for a watering can when she arrived at the shed. "No one will think less of you if you aren't on the fire team. In fact, I think they'd all rather know if you have doubts. You could end up getting everyone killed if they're all depending on you and you can't go through with something."

Charity picked up the bags of seeds and stared at them blankly. "Still, I think I should train. We might get in a situation where I don't have a choice. I may have to fight." She looked up at Ava. "Every one of you have had to take a life. You, Foley, your dad; even James. He shot that guy who was trying to rob us. How did you know? Did you always feel that you would be able to kill someone if it came down to your life or theirs?"

"No. When I bought my pistol, when we took the concealed carry class, I had a pretty good idea that I could. But I didn't know for sure until I had to do it." Ava remembered the incident on the bridge. Her heart raced almost as if she were standing there now. She took a deep breath and held it to calm herself. "But the guy who was holding me in the house; I had no question. I knew if I got a chance, I was going to take it. It wasn't any easier, but I knew I wouldn't hesitate."

Ava's eyebrows slanted up remorsefully and her chin lowered. "And about the bridge . . ."

"It's alright. You had no choice. You saved our lives." Charity put her hand on Ava's arm.

"No, it's not that. We promised to never talk about it to anyone. I told my dad. And I told Foley."

Charity hugged her. "They needed to know. James and I figured you'd told them."

"Thanks for understanding."

"Thanks for saving our lives." Charity gave her one more squeeze before letting go and returning to the garden beds. "But if you don't mind, let's keep my insecurities between us for now. I want to train with you guys. If a mission comes up and I don't think I can handle it, I'll bow out, I promise."

"Sounds like a good plan." Ava walked beside her with the watering can. "Who knows, the training may give you the confidence you need."

After lunch, everyone made their way out to the shooting mound, including Sam and Betty. Foley and Ulysses had spent the morning constructing targets out of paper and wood salvaged off pallets. They'd arranged the targets in a sort of shooting obstacle course.

Foley waved his hand and instructed everyone to come to where he was standing. "Target shooting is great, but it doesn't accurately emulate an actual combat situation. Of course, nothing really feels like combat except combat. But, we can improve our odds of surviving a shootout by training to shoot and move at the same time. Because in an actual firefight, that's your only hope."

Ulysses handed radios to Ava, James, and Charity. "You three are going to be up first. Put the radio's earpiece in your ear, run the cord under your shirt and attach the radio to the back of your waist, so it's not in the way. What we'll be doing today is training to shoot, move, and communicate. Each of you will take your own lane of fire. I'm going to call out instructions to each of you individually. You'll take the action I tell you, then go down to one knee until I give you your next command. This will get you guys used to listening to radio traffic and picking out the instructions from your team leader which are intended for you. You'll get used to having someone else shooting beside you, and you'll get familiar with shooting and moving at the same time.

"When you move, keep your feet spread at least shoulder-width apart, never cross your feet when moving side to side, and keep your feet even farther apart when moving backward. The last thing you want to do in a firefight is trip, particularly over your own feet."

Ava nodded. "Ready."

Charity took the center lane. "Me, too!"

"Let's do it." James held his rifle at low-ready

position.

Ulysses held the radio and began giving each of them a few simple instructions. "Ava, walk toward your first target and fire three shots."

Ava leveled her rifle, kept her feet wide as she moved forward. Pop, pop, pop.

"Charity, take a shot, run up to Ava's position, and fire three more." Charity fired once, then hustled up to where Ava was, then took three more shots.

"Remember, take a knee when you've completed your task," Ulysses called.

James followed his directives, then Ulysses called out another round of instructions. He gradually pushed the instructions closer together and made them more complicated. He reminded the shooters to keep their feet farther apart several times throughout the course.

Once they'd finished, Sam and Betty took the radios.

Ava took a seat by a tree next to Foley. "How did I do?"

"You did great. I was thinking about that hog that got into the compost."

Ava looked at her rifle. "It would be nice to kill it, right?"

"Yeah, but it would be even better to trap it."

"Let me guess. It would be even better to trap two."

He smiled. "Or three."

"Do you think they'll breed in captivity?"

"Feral hogs are just domestic hogs that got loose at some point. I doubt they're very selective about how or where they breed."

Ava chuckled. "Reminds me of a girl Charity and I used to work with."

"Hogs would add variety to our diet. If this thing goes on too long, I doubt we'll be able to count on the grocery stores."

"I agree. Did you talk to my dad about going out to Marble Falls tomorrow?"

"I did."

Ava looked him in the eyes. "And he wants to go but he doesn't want to take me."

Foley turned his attention toward Betty and Sam as they progressed through the shooting course. "That's about the size of it."

"Well, I'm going. He's just going to have to get used to it." Ava stood up. "Come on, I want to run the course with you beside me."

Foley pushed off the tree. "Feel like running it with AKs this time?"

"Sure."

# CHAPTER 10

But seek ye first the kingdom of God, and his righteousness; and all these things shall be added unto you.

Matthew 6:33

Sunday morning, Foley organized an informal Bible study on the back deck. He read several passages about David when he was being hunted down by King Saul and applied it to the group's situation. He explained how God had protected and sustained David while being pursued by an overwhelming military force and a government leader who wanted him dead.

Afterward, James said the closing prayer.

Betty stood up before anyone left the back deck. "Ulysses and Foley, I know you fellas want to make a run to the store, but I'd be very grateful if you'd wait until after lunch. Sunday has always been fried chicken and biscuits around here. Sam killed two hens before breakfast so we'd have plenty, but if y'all run off, I can't guarantee there will be any leftovers. I hate to toot my own horn, but folks have trouble controlling themselves over my fried chicken."

Foley held Ava's hand and looked at Ulysses.

"You want to wait, don't you?" Ulysses asked.

"If it was anything but fried chicken, sir." Foley's eyes begged him to delay the expedition.

Ulysses conceded with a nod. "Fried chicken does sound good. And I wouldn't mind watching the Sunday morning shows. I'm sure they'll be laying it on thick today."

Ava followed her father into the house toward the living room. "And don't try to leave without me. I'm coming along!"

"So I've heard." Ulysses continued to the couch and clicked on the television.

Charity assisted Betty. The others gathered around the television.

Sunday morning talk show host, Ophelia Martin, sat opposite Hollywood actor and self-proclaimed voice of Antifa, Shane Lawrence.

"Shane, we extended an invitation to billionaire business mogul George Szabos, but his office referred us to you. I think everyone knows that you and Mr. Szabos are close, but it was as if he was implying that you speak for him."

Lawrence laughed. "Ophelia, George is his own

man, and so am I, but we're on the same page, especially when it comes to America. I don't suppose I'm overstepping my bounds if I tell you that George is a very close advisor to the administration. And I'm sure it's no surprise the amount of preparation President Markovich is having to make. We've never had such a tumultuous transition in the history of this country."

Ophelia Martin shook her head. "I do not envy President Markovich. But if anyone is up to the challenge of bringing this divided country back together it's him."

Lawrence nodded. "Well said, Ophelia."

Sam Hodge crossed his arms. "You couldn't pry the word *president* out of any of these puppets for the last eight years. It was always *Higgins this* or *Higgins that*. Same thing for the few short days that Ross was president. But Markovich is still seven weeks away from taking the oath and they're already calling him President Markovich."

No one else commented but continued listening to the interview.

Ophelia leaned in. "What are your thoughts on the legitimacy of the states that have declared themselves to be free and independent from the federal government?"

Lawrence chuckled. "I can call myself the Queen of England but that's not going to get me past the guard gate at Buckingham Palace. I don't mean to make light of a serious situation, but come on!

"And what the so-called Alliance States are

doing is far worse. If I have a particular delusion that affects only myself, that's not so bad. But we have a small handful of people, like Turner Blackwell, a smattering of rogue governors, and the arrogantly-named Liberty Caucus who have the audacity to claim they speak for everyone in their respective states." Shane Lawrence held out his hands as if to plead his case. "They don't! Look, Ophelia, this would be comical if it didn't have the possibility of encouraging the sort of people who are already emotionally unstable. My argument is that Blackwell and his cohorts are dangerous. Much more dangerous than any terrorist organization our country has ever had to contend with. We need calmer heads to prevail before someone gets hurt. If that doesn't happen, the kid gloves are going to come off.

"They may think they have until January to play this little charade with our leader, but this insanity isn't going to be tolerated."

Ophelia cupped the arms of her grey upholstered swivel chair. "Interim President Woods is close with the Markovich administration. He was on the short list for VP as we all remember. Is it safe to say Maximillian Markovich has his ear? And if so, does that present any legal hurdles? Blackwell has made many inflammatory statements calling the arrangement a quote, *puppet regime.*"

Lawrence shook his head dismissively. "Every administration has a transition period where the president-elect and his staff work in lockstep with the out-going team. The special nature of how Interim President Woods came to the oval office has no bearing on that protocol."

"That's fair." Ophelia nodded her approval. She hesitated before her next question. Her face took on a grave expression before continuing. Her lips tightened and her brows lowered. "I suppose we should dispense with the little dance we're doing around the elephant in the room." Her artificially pained eyes gazed upon Shane Lawrence. "I hope this is nothing more than a superfluous thought experiment on my part, but let's suppose the worst happens. Rumors are already flying around about members of the armed services who are abandoning their post to join up with Blackwell. It's come out that while Ross was being tried, Secretary of Defense Albert Domingo began moving troops and equipment to states that have since joined Blackwell's alliance. I'm confident that President Markovich will deal with this situation in a fair and diplomatic manner, but what about the poor souls who are caught in the crossfire? Millions of honest, hardworking citizens, many of whom voted for President-elect Markovich, are essentially trapped in these locations where the leadership is declaring themselves to be . . . enemy combatants, for lack of a better word."

Lawrence nodded emphatically. "You couldn't have found a better label. Treasonous traitors perhaps, but the term *enemy combatants* describes them perfectly. In fact, Mr. Domingo has earned his own private cell in Guantanamo Bay. He's getting checked in as we speak."

Ophelia titled. "Rather ironic when you consider how hard he fought to keep it open."

Lawrence applauded her pointed jest with a quick clap of the hands and an exaggerated laugh. "Don't you love karma?"

"It has a way of making its rounds." She angled her chin up and gave a venomous smile.

"It sure does, Ophelia. But let me answer your question about the innocent people who are at risk of being caught in the middle of all this. Like you, I fully trust that the president will reach a peaceful resolution. But on the off chance that he can't, if reason refuses to be heard by Blackwell, there are systems in place to separate the wheat from the chaff."

"I'm intrigued! Tell me more."

"We have to be careful about revealing methods and tactics." Lawrence acted as if he weren't going to elaborate, but then suddenly capitulated. "But if you insist. It's actually two separate systems. When we're talking about people's freedom, we need redundancy. The first, as you might have guessed, is social media. Whether you're a supporter of Markovich or Ross, everything you say online is recorded. Even deleted posts can be brought up from the depths of the social media servers. But this is a human problem and it needs the delicate touch of a person to dig deeper. For that, I'm pleased to announce that I've had the opportunity to work directly with the administration and George Szabos in putting together a network of concerned citizens who will be the eyes and ears of the president."

"Congratulations! I had no idea you had been given a formal role in all of this. You are so modest and humble. Why didn't you say something earlier?"

Ava fumed. "The network already knew about this! Why else would they have some loud-mouthed Hollywood actor on the most-watched political talk show when the nation is on the precipice of civil war. What a phony display they've cooked up for us!"

Lawrence continued. "It's not about me, Ophelia. I'm honored to be a part of it, but this is bigger than Shane Lawrence."

"Can you tell us the name of the organization? Who will be involved?"

"It's called the Social Justice Legion."

"Sounds familiar. Is this an evolution of the Social Justice Warriors League?"

"Yes, but much stronger. George's Just Society Foundation is fostering the development of the program, just as he sponsored the inception and growth of the SJWL. We've also brought the good folks from the Social Justice Law Center on board. The SJLC will be advising us on developing protocols for going through social media posts to determine who in the military is a friend and who might be best treated as a potential foe.

"Obviously a derogatory Facebook post about President Markovich isn't necessarily get you tossed into a re-education camp, but I think it was Confucius who said 'out of the overflow of the heart, the mouth speaks.'"

"I'm pretty sure that was Jesus who coined that

phrase, you ignorant pinhead!" Ava shook her fist at the TV.

"I'm all for finding out who is with us and who is against us, Ophelia. We need that kind of information and the people who will be tasked with auditing social media posts will be doing an invaluable service as they classify dissidents into low, medium, and high-risk domestic threats.

"But you know me. I'm a brass-tacks kind of guy. Like the roles I play in Hollywood, I like action. So the Social Justice Legion is also bringing in people from the Antifa movement; you know, to give it some teeth."

Ophelia covered her mouth as if to contain her glee. "Turner Blackwell doesn't know what he's up against. It sounds like a revolution for the people, by the people."

Foley voiced his objection. "It sounds like the Nazi Brown Shirts."

"It sounds like every communist revolution that's come before," Ulysses added.

"Lunch is ready. Y'all get on in here to the table," Betty called.

Ava's stomach was soured from listening to the scripted rhetoric being passed off as an informal discussion. She figured that was how it was done in communist countries so she'd best get used to it for a while. America had taken decades to descend to this level of radical socialism. The damage would not be undone overnight. For now, she needed her strength, so she purposed to forget about the distasteful dialogue and focus on the delectable aroma coming from the kitchen.

# CHAPTER 11

He that is slow to anger is better than the mighty; and he that ruleth his spirit than he that taketh a city.

Proverbs 16:32

Ava walked off the porch of Sam Hodge's farmhouse and handed her rifle to Ulysses. He tucked it neatly under the back seat of his truck with his and Foley's weapons.

Ulysses opened the driver's side door. "Foley, would you mind riding in the back? If we get in a pinch, it would be good to have someone who can access the rifles."

"Sure." The back door creaked as Foley closed it.

"We could keep the rifles in the seats beside us."

Ava got in the front of the truck.

"This truck . . . isn't exactly registered and insured." Ulysses closed his door. "We don't want to create any additional negative attention by having rifles out where folks driving by could see them."

"Why don't we take Foley's truck?" she asked.

"That would defeat the purpose of having an unregistered vehicle." Ulysses started the engine. "Do you have an extra magazine for your pistol?"

She patted her back pocket. "Yes."

Buckley chased the truck down the driveway, barking and wagging his tail.

Ava called out the window to her dog, "I'll be right back, Buck."

She rolled up her window and looked over at her father. "Thanks for bringing me with you."

Ulysses tightened his jaw. "Last time, I tried to leave you at home so you'd be safe. That didn't work out so well."

Ava turned around to smile at Foley. "We survived."

Ulysses said, "You were in good hands."

"Better hands with both of us here," Foley added.

The twenty-minute drive out toward Marble Falls was uneventful until shortly after they'd turned north on 281. Suddenly, six Marble Falls Police Department cars zoomed past them, lights and sirens filling the air with the sights and sounds of a hazardous event.

"I wonder what that's all about?" Ava watched as the patrol cars raced by.

"I don't know," Foley said. "But it looks like the

entire department."

Shortly thereafter, a train of four vehicles from the Burnet County Sherriff's Department sped by.

Ava looked on. "Whatever it is, at least it's in the other direction."

Ulysses continued to the Walmart where they'd planned to purchase as many supplies as they could carry back in the bed of the truck. He parked near the back of the lot. "Hats and sunglasses. Remember, you're on camera."

"We're not doing anything wrong." Ava tucked her hair into her ball cap and pulled it low over her eyes.

"You're a conservative. You heard the news this morning. That's a crime." Ulysses stepped out of the truck and adjusted his shirt to cover his pistol.

Ava looked Foley over as he got out.

"How do I look?" he asked.

"Cute." She smiled.

"Thanks. But can you see my pistol? I've got my .45 under my shirt."

She took his hand. "No. You're good."

They collected shopping carts as they neared the entrance. Five Hispanic men wearing baggy pants and long tee-shirts stood by the front doors. All of the men were heavily tattooed, most had tattoos on their face. One stepped forward lifting his shirt to reveal the pearl handle of a very ornate gold-plated .45. "Sorry vato, we close today."

Ulysses smiled and nodded. "Okay, we'll come back later." He pushed the cart to the side and turned around. "Back to the truck. Stay in front of me."

Ava's eyes opened wide at the sight of the gang member brandishing his weapon. She said nothing but complied with her father's instructions. Foley also turned around without talking and put his shoulder behind Ava's back.

Once they'd passed several cars and were out of earshot of the thugs, Ava asked, "What are we going to do?"

"Nothing. We're going home." Ulysses walked close behind her. "The police and sheriff's department were probably responding to a make-believe threat on the other side of town. The gang likely called in a hostage situation on the other side of town as a diversion. I'm guessing ninety percent of the available law enforcement are at least twenty minutes away from here."

She turned to look at him. "We can't let them get away with this!"

"Of course we can," Ulysses replied matter-of-factly.

"If these guys decide Marble Falls is a soft target, they'll take it over," she contested.

"Not our problem."

"It will be if we have to go all the way to Fredericksburg to get supplies."

Ulysses exhaled heavily to show his displeasure with the situation.

"She's right," Foley said.

"If we do this town a favor, maybe they'll help us out someday." Ava slowed her pace as they approached the truck.

Ulysses unlocked the truck. "Get in. Foley, pass the rifles up to the front."

"We're going to fight?" Ava grew ecstatic.

"No. We're going to leave. We'll keep driving and find the next town with a grocery store."

Ava took her rifle from Foley. "Then why are we getting out the big guns?"

"In case we happen to cross paths with them on our way out. Listen, Ava, even if I was with an eight-man squad of highly-trained, well-armed soldiers, I'd walk away from this one. We don't know how many more of them are inside. We don't know if they have more scouts set up as an over-watch team. Way too many variables and unknowns."

"What about the golden rule? Wouldn't you want someone to help us out if we were in a bad spot?" She positioned her rifle and rolled down her window in case she had to engage.

"No. That's the other thing. The store is full of innocent bystanders. Even if we're able to take out all the gang members, the odds of us hitting non-combatants is ridiculously high. It's unacceptable. The best thing we can do for ourselves and the people inside is walk away." Ulysses checked the map on his phone before driving off. "When my team would plan an operation, we'd train for weeks. We'd learn everything we could about the buildings, terrain, weapons, and personnel. We'd hit them when they were the weakest. And still, with all the planning we did, things still went wrong."

Ava sat silently as Ulysses found a back road to get them out of town and away from the disturbance. Other than his acknowledgment that Ava's assessment was accurate, Foley managed to stay out of the disagreement between Ava and her father. She didn't fault him for it. In fact, she recognized the wisdom in his restraint. And though she hated to let the wolves prey upon the shoppers at the Marble Falls Walmart, she also accepted Ulysses course of action as prudent.

Ulysses glanced at the rearview. "Ever been to Kingsland?"

"No," Foley replied.

"Me, either." Ava watched the rearview for trouble.

"It's only about another ten miles. They've got a grocery. We'll get what we can."

When they arrived at the small market in Kingsland, Texas, Ulysses parked at the rear of the lot. After scanning the parking lot for souped-up lowriders, Ava and Ulysses passed their rifles to Foley to stow under the back seat.

"Hats on. Avoid eye contact and only speak when spoken too." Ulysses stepped out of the truck and closed the door.

Ava and Foley followed him through the entrance doors of the grocery. Ava kept her eyes peeled for anything unusual. The first item of interest to catch her attention was the pump-action shotgun leaning up against the register. She made an effort to not stare and grabbed a cart.

Ulysses led the way down the first aisle. He began filling his cart with pasta and cans of sauce. He quickly emptied the canned sauces from the shelf and began carefully gathering several glass jars of sauce.

Ava looked at her father. "Sam and Betty have

made some room in their freezer since we arrived. I'm going to stock up on meat. I'll see you guys over there."

"Good idea, but let's stick together." Ulysses seemed satisfied with his haul of pasta and sauce.

"Okay." Ava waited, then pushed her cart to the butcher's section in the back of the store. She looked through the window where a man was packaging more meat. He wore a leather belt with a long-barreled revolver in the holster. Ava looked at Foley who had also spotted the armed butcher. Neither of them spoke.

Ulysses began piling stacks of beef into Ava's cart. Ava selected several packages of pork, while Foley focused on restocking breakfast sausage and bacon. Next, they hit the coffee aisle, nearly filing an entire cart. The store only had six large bags of rice, so they took all of them. That cart was topped off with the lion's share of the store's dried bean selection.

"We'll need to make two trips," Ulysses said as he pushed the heavy cart. "We'll check out, then come back for another haul."

"I'll stay outside and watch the truck." Foley shoved the grocery cart which was laden down with rice and beans.

"I appreciate that." Ulysses worked his way to the checkout counter and began unloading his cart.

The cashier was an older lady with grizzled hair. Her voice sounded like she preferred non-filtered cigarettes and her eyes looked like they belonged to someone who wouldn't hesitate to empty that shotgun leaning up against her register. "I reckon y'all come from the city. Hear tell ain't many grocers open in San Antonio; Austin neither. Lots of folks stockin' up. Truck just left a while ago. Lucky for y'all. By the time we closed last night, could have fit about everything we had left on the shelves in them three carts y'all got."

She continued scanning the items and looked at Ulysses' face. "What happened to your eye?"

"Accident."

She nodded suspiciously and scanned the remaining groceries from Ulysses' cart. Without looking back up, she asked, "Did you get that scar down your lip in the same accident?"

"Same one." Ulysses didn't elaborate.

She glanced at her shotgun and proceeded to run the groceries from Ava's cart across the scanner. "Can't be too careful. Bunch of ne'er-do-wells came through Blanco yesterday, robbin' grocery stores of all things. Sister lives down there. Said it was Mexican gangs; Tango Blast or some such foolishness. I ain't never heard of gangs robbin' grocery stores. They get all that money selling meth and runnin' whores. Don't make no sense."

She quickly scanned the rice and beans from Foley's cart, then looked at the sales total indicator on the register and watched as Ulysses pulled out a roll of one-hundred-dollar bills. The woman looked at the store manager standing by the door holding a bolt-action hunting rifle. He looked to be in his late fifties with a balding head. "Collin thinks that devil, Markovich, is sending them gangs into all the small towns to give us a hard time. Ain't none of us voted for him. All I can say is he best not send nobody to come get my shotgun. They might get it, but they'll have to take it bullets first."

Ava made a conscious effort not to look at the woman, but she couldn't help but crack a grin at the woman's determination and wit.

"We're coming back for few more items after we get this out to the truck." Ulysses handed her the money and waited for her to count out the change. "If that's okay."

"Suit yourself. If we sell out of everything, I can go home early."

The load was quickly transferred into the bed of the truck. Foley waited outside while Ava and Ulysses went in for a second round. Once the two carts were filled to capacity, they returned to the register. Ava paid for the follow-up run. She let the old woman chatter away, but followed Ulysses' instructions and kept quiet. Having been spoken to, Ava said, "Have a blessed day," as she pushed her cart out the door. She smiled politely at the manager while they exited. Ava saw no harm in that.

# CHAPTER 12

And Samuel told all the words of the Lord unto the people that asked of him a king. And he said, This will be the manner of the king that shall reign over you: He will take your sons, and appoint them for himself, for his chariots, and to be his horsemen; and some shall run before his chariots. And he will appoint him captains over thousands, and captains over fifties; and will set them to ear his ground, and to reap his harvest, and to make his instruments of war, and instruments of his chariots. And he will take your daughters to be confectionaries, and to be cooks, and to be bakers. And he will take your fields, and your vineyards, and your oliveyards, even the best of them, and give them to his servants. And he will take the tenth of your seed, and of your vineyards, and give to his officers, and to his servants. And he will take your menservants, and your maidservants, and your goodliest young men, and your asses, and put them to his work. He will take the tenth of your sheep: and ye shall be his servants. And ye shall cry out in that day because of your king which ye shall have chosen you; and the Lord will not hear you in that day.

1 Samuel 8:10-18

Ava sat at the kitchen counter Monday morning, checking the news on her computer. Charity helped Betty prepare breakfast for everyone. Ulysses sat next to Ava, sipping a cup of coffee. Foley sat on the other side of her, looking on at her computer screen. Sam was in the FROG, keeping watch. And James was sleeping, having been on watch the night prior.

Ava said, "Woods just signed a temporary firearm's ban. Congress had it waiting on his desk this morning."

"I saw that coming." Ulysses took another drink of his coffee.

"Why bother calling it temporary?" Betty tended to the sausage patties sizzling in the pan.

Foley spun around on his stool. "I'm sure

Markovich will want to sign a permanent ban after the inauguration. Otherwise, the ban doesn't get credited to his administration. It's all about legacy."

Ava continued to read the article. "They're claiming the ban was rushed through in an emergency session. Supposedly, Congress is trying to curb violence stemming from disagreements over the states who have declared themselves independent."

Charity cracked eggs into a skillet. "Do you think the ban will apply to Antifa, MS-13 and Tango Blast?"

"Not a chance." Ava shook her head. "Antifa has been co-opted by the government as part of the Social Justice Legion. And since most of the weapons in the hands of MS-13 and Tango Blast came from the DOJ via Fast and Furious, they're probably exempt."

"So basically, it's just conservatives who can't be trusted with firearms." Betty put the sausage patties on a plate with a paper towel to absorb the grease.

"Now you're catching on." Ava scrolled through the news.

Ulysses stood to refill his cup. "We should stash some weapons. I'm sure the government will eventually go door-to-door collecting firearms."

"I'm with Ma Kettle back at the grocery store. If they want mine, they'll have to take them bullets first," Ava said defiantly.

Ulysses nodded slowly. "In theory, I'm with you. But that isn't practical nor effective. When they come, they'll come with an overwhelming force. If we shoot it out with them, we'll take a few with us, but we'll all be dead when the smoke clears. It makes much more sense to hand over a few guns, let them go on their way, then dig up our real arsenal after they've gone. Afterward, we launch an insurgency attack from the shadows."

Ava looked at Foley. "What do you think?"

"Jihadists kept the American military running in circles for well over a decade with that tactic. If they'd have hit us head-on, it would have been no contest. We'd have crushed them in a matter of days. Your dad is right."

"Do we have what we need to do that?" Ava turned to her father.

"Sam has a FoodSaver vacuum sealer. We can double bag our ammo and firearms with that. It'll be airtight and watertight so we can bury them. It would be nice to have some large-diameter PVC pipe to keep the FoodSaver bags from being pierced accidentally, but as long as we're careful, the weapons should be fine."

Ava replied, "Good to know, but that's not what I meant. Do we have the materials we need to launch an insurgency campaign?"

"We don't have RPGs, grenades, or explosives if that's what you mean."

"They sell that stuff on the dark web."

Ulysses chuckled. "You're not talking about a quarter bag of weed. People don't just ship that kind of thing to your door. You have to meet dealers in person."

"Okay, if that's how it's done." Ava lifted her shoulders.

"No, no." Ulysses shook his head. "These guys get set up and taken out by ATF all the time. Once they take down a darknet dealer, they use his online profile to make controlled sales to other buyers. A dealer could have a perfect rating on Hidden Wiki and still, it's a fifty-fifty shot that he's an agent.

"Even with the darknet, the only way to make a purchase like that is through someone you know."

"What about Antifa? You know them," Ava said.

"I've stalked their hangouts online. I've never made contact with anyone and never intended to. My profile for the message board and Blackbook is a girl, remember? Even if I could set up a meeting, a sixty-year-old man with a lazy eye and a scar down his jaw isn't exactly who they'd expect to show up."

Ava bit her lower lip and stared at her father.

His head shook from side to side slowly, then faster. "Nope, absolutely not, Ava. Quit thinking it."

"Why not?"

"A million reasons why not. We'll be here all day if I start telling you why not."

"Top ten."

Ulysses gritted his teeth. "Number one reason; the only one that matters—the best-laid plans of mice and men."

"Often go awry." She finished the saying.

"Exactly. The internet didn't exist back then, but this is what I did for a living. My last mission was perfectly orchestrated, planned to the T, everybody who was anybody had been paid off. We bought green lights and hall passes to get us all the way from Moscow to Beijing, yet I still missed out on being a father to my little girl because the perfect plan failed."

Ava felt sorry for the man sitting beside her. She felt sorry for herself. She wondered if all the pain and heartache of growing up without a dad could have been averted. If only Ulysses had cashed in his chips on the mission prior. What might have her life been like? She sighed. *What a futile endeavor to consider what might have been. It is what it is, and we have to make the most with what we have to work with.*

"Y'all get to the table. Breakfast is ready," Betty called.

After breakfast, Ava took her computer up to her room. She booted the TAILS operating system which she'd downloaded from her father's flash drive. She launched the TOR browser and navigated to Blackbook. She hesitated before logging in with her father's credentials for his Harley Quinn profile, but not for long. Once inside, she'd crossed the Rubicon. Turning back was not an option.

Ava spent the next two hours surreptitiously reading all of Harley Quinn's posts and threads. She put herself in the shoes of this fictitious character, trying to guess how Harley would respond to threads and posts before actually reading Quinn's comments.

A knock came to the door. Ava panicked and slammed the laptop shut.

Charity stuck her head in the door. "What are you doing in here all alone?"

"Nothing," Ava said much too emphatically.

"Oh." Charity's eyebrows tugged toward one another. She looked around the room skeptically. "Well, when you're finished doing nothing, why don't you come downstairs. The guys built a pen to trap pigs. You and I have been tasked with catching some fish so we can use the guts for bait."

"I'll be right down." Ava sat with her forearms on the closed laptop.

Charity inspected the bedroom one last time before closing the door.

Ava took a deep breath, relieved at not being interrogated further. Her clandestine operation would not be approved by her father. She could not put Foley at odds with Ulysses by sharing the information with him, and Charity wouldn't share her sense of urgency nor understand why this mission was so critical. At least for the planning stages, Ava was on her own. Once everything was in place, she'd share details on a need-to-know basis. But for now, no one else needed to know.


"You're a million miles away." Charity reeled in her lure and recast.

"What?" Ava ignored her bobber floating lifelessly into the grass near the bank.

"What's on your mind?"

"Nothing, just being quiet so we don't scare the fish."

"They can't hear us."

Ava reeled in her line and picked a tuft of grass from the hook. She sent the lure hurtling through the air, hoping it would stay where it landed so she wouldn't need to keep recasting. Her mind was occupied with more important matters. *ZZZZzzzzz.* Her reel began spinning.

"You got one!" Charity cheered.

Ava set the hook and began slowly bringing the fish in. "How many do we need to bait the trap?"

"It's supposed to be for our dinner also, so quite a few more than one." Charity watched as Ava brought the fish up out of the water, removed it from the hook and dropped it into the bucket of river water. "Obviously you don't want to talk about it right now, but whenever you're ready, I'm here."

Ava knew what that meant. Charity would passive-aggressively hound her until she spilled the beans. She sent her lure back out to trick another fish into the frying pan. Ava willed herself to put her secret objective on the back burner for a while, to be present, and engage with Charity. "Oh, you know how it is. Our whole world is upside down. I guess I've been so caught up in the activities of it all that I haven't realized the gravity of everything. I suppose it just hit me all of a sudden today."

Charity furrowed her brow. "I know what you mean." Charity's bobber went under. "I think I've got a bite!"

Two hours later, the girls had seven good-sized bass from the river. Ava grabbed the bucket and her rod. "This is enough for dinner. Let's clean them so we can eat."

After dinner, Ava was up for night watch. She welcomed the time alone with her thoughts, having nothing else to do except stare through a rifle scope and concoct her devious scheme.

# CHAPTER 13

Like as a father pitieth his children, so the Lord pitieth them that fear him. For he knoweth our frame; he remembereth that we are dust.

Psalm 103:13-14

Before sunrise on Wednesday morning, Ava was abruptly ripped from a state of deep slumber. Her bedroom door flew open. Instinctively, she rolled out from beneath the covers and onto the floor between the bed and the wall. She stuck her hand on her nightstand and grabbed her 1911.

The lights came on and she heard her father's voice. "Ava! What have you done?"

Ava let the pistol drop to the floor. The sound of

utter disappointment pierced her soul. Her shoulders slumped. "Why are you up so early? What time is it?" She looked over the side of the bed with one eye squinted.

Ulysses closed the door. "Answer the question, Ava." The tone in his voice was one of deep emotional loss, not of anger. She could've handled anger. But not this; not hurt—knowing she was the source of his pain.

Ava kept her gaze low, both because her eyes were still adjusting to the light and because she dared not look him in the eye. She placed the gun back on the nightstand and crawled up on the bed.

Ulysses took a seat at the foot of the bed. "I saw the conversation you initiated in the message board using Harley's profile. No one else had my login credentials. Please don't make this worse by lying."

"One of the guys you message regularly, I think his screen name is Chewy2K, he seems to have gotten a hold of some military grade explosives; PBX. From what I gather, lots of *toys* are being shuffled out the back door and being turned over to the higher-ups within the Social Justice Legion. The group is recognized by the Markovich regime and no formal regulatory guidelines have come out to advise them on what is considered proper conduct. I assume this gray area is intentional and it's open season on conservatives.

"Anyway, I guess the Antifa contacts in Austin have so many goodies they don't know what to do with it all. They're offering some of it for sale to like-minded comrades. I was just curious how much stuff like that was going for."

"You set up a buy, Ava. That's not just curious. How did you intend to pay for it?"

"I've got cash. Quite a bit of it."

Ulysses shook his head. "These guys don't usually want cash."

"Then what do they want?"

"Monero, or Litecoin. But usually Monero."

"Isn't Monero like Bitcoin?"

"Yes, but harder to track. It still uses blockchain technology to verify transactions, but it's passed through a network of shell wallets to make tracing nearly impossible. Monero is to Bitcoin what Tor is to Internet Explorer."

"If I have to convert my cash, I'll find a way to do it. Austin has people who sell Bitcoins for cash. I'm sure I can find someone who'll sell me Monero for cash."

"How do you know about buying Bitcoins for cash?"

"Some girl I used to work with at Dr. Hodge's. She bought Bitcoins from people in Austin for a premium. She used it to buy drugs online. She said she was afraid they'd track her if she bought her Bitcoins online using a bank account."

"Well, it doesn't matter. You're not making the buy. And after I back out of the deal, that will be the end of my contacts with Antifa. I'm not trying to shame you or make you feel guilty, but you have to realize when you make unilateral decisions like that, it has consequences that affect everyone on your team."

Ava let her eyes glance upward only momentarily. "I'm sorry. But considering everything we stand to lose, maybe you should think about going through with it. At least you know about it now. You can plan the operation. I'll do everything you tell me to do. I'll follow your instructions to the letter."

"I'm not having this conversation!" Ulysses stood up. "I'm hurt, disappointed. But you're pushing me toward anger. Drop the subject and don't bring it up again."

"Yes, sir." She folded her hands contritely.

"I'll talk to you later today. I haven't been to sleep yet."

"Sleep well. I'm sorry, I never wanted to disappoint you. I'm just very afraid that if we don't take advantage of every opportunity, we'll lose Texas. And if Texas falls, the rest of America is going to topple like a chain of dominos; even the Alliance States. I hope I haven't cost us the war. Without that information from inside the Antifa camp, we're effectively flying blind.

"And my mind went wild with all the possibilities we'd have if I could get that PBX. Chewy says he has remote detonators and everything. But I'm sorry."

Ulysses stood in the doorway tight-jawed, as if it pained him to walk away from this deal. "It's okay. I forgive you."

"One more thing before you go." Ava pulled the comforter up to her shoulders.

"What's that?" Ulysses paused.

"I love you. I guess I should have told you sooner, I've felt it since the moment I knew you were my dad, but it just seemed . . . weird."

He looked like he was choking back tears. "I love you, too, sweetheart. Even before I knew if you were a boy or a girl. All that time, sitting in that prison, thinking about you as a little baby, I loved you all that time. And that's why we're not doing this deal." He turned out the lights and closed the door.

"Wow! She's a big one." Ava reached over the side of the pen late Wednesday morning.

"I wouldn't do that if I were you." Foley grabbed her hand and jerked it back. "She can crack pecans and hickory nuts with those teeth. Your fingers wouldn't stand a chance."

The wild pig squealed and grunted as it twisted around in circles, frantically seeking an exit.

"Oh! I didn't know they would bite."

"A caged chipmunk will bite. An angry hog will tear you up."

Ava shuddered, erasing the savage vision of being eaten by a feral hog from her mind. "So now we have two females and no male."

"You've got to catch some more fish so we can reset the trap. Maybe tonight will be our night. I'm sure your dad would enjoy fishing with you again."

"I don't know about that." Ava sighed.

"Why would you say that?"

Ava gave Foley the details of her covert plot to obtain explosives.

Foley shook his head, his mouth hanging open wider than his astonished eyes. "I can't believe you! Do you realize how dangerous that would have been?"

"Foley! We're basically going to war against the most powerful military in the history of the earth. That's like jumping out of a plane without a parachute while lecturing me about running with scissors."

"Not quite," he contested. "We're talking calculated risks."

"Yeah, going up against the US military is a calculated risk."

"It's not all of the military. More than a third have either defected to the Alliance States or were stationed there already and have fallen in under Blackwell's command."

She rolled her eyes. "Okay, since we're only going up against two-thirds of the US military, that's a calculated risk. And spare me the scolding. I've already been tarred and feathered by my dad."

Foley rubbed his forehead. "What's done is done. But next time, talk to me first. I want you to know you can trust me."

"I do trust you, Foley. But involving you would have put you and my father at odds. I don't want that."

"Thanks, but it won't matter if you get yourself killed."

"It's war. That's what people do." Ava stomped toward the house.

"Where are you off to?" Foley tagged along.

She huffed. "To get my fishing pole. It's the only thing people think I'm good for around here."

Charity met them at the deck. "Hey guys, the news is on. You should hear what they're talking about."

Ava turned to Foley. "Can you go wake my dad up? He's sleeping in his trailer. If it's something important he'll want to know what's going on."

"Sure." He turned to go back.

"And Foley," she said before he left.

"Yes?"

"I'm sorry I snapped. I get a little defensive when I screw up. That's something I'm working on."

"All is forgiven." He winked and continued his quest.

Ava followed Charity to the television. "What's going on?"

"The Senate confirmed all of Woods' Cabinet appointments."

"Let me guess, they're all from Markovich's short list." Ava plopped down on the couch.

Charity sat next to James who was already in the room.

Betty sat in Sam's recliner. "How did you guess?" she asked facetiously.

"Par for the course," Ava replied.

Charity elaborated on the situation. "The new Secretary of Defense and the new Secretary of Homeland Security are going to give a joint press conference. The media is speculating as to what it will be about. Everyone seems to think it will cover the Alliance States and what action DC will take against them. Some think they'll talk about the gun ban."

Ava bit her lip in anticipation.

Foley hurried in and was soon followed by a crazy-looking Ulysses. When he was groggy, his lazy eye gave him a disoriented appearance. And while it had frightened Ava before she knew him, she now saw it as cute; evoking feelings of endearment toward the man.

Foley sat on one side of Ava and Ulysses on the other.

The television broadcast an image from the White House Press Briefing Room. Woods' Press Secretary stepped to the podium. "Thank you all for coming. President Woods will be meeting with all of the new Cabinet members later this evening to welcome them. Today is going to be a big day, so we won't have time for many questions, but you will be hearing from a few of the new senior officials in the President's Cabinet.

"Allow me to welcome to the podium, a man who you already know since he has been acting Secretary of Defense, filling the vacancy until his appointment could be formalized, Ryan Coleman. Also the new head of DHS, Secretary Alexander Douglas."

Coleman approached the podium with Douglas standing at his flank. "Thank you."

A barrage of flashes from cameras persisted for more than a minute then finally subsided. "Thank you all for coming. As you all know, the trouble we've had with Governor Blackwell and several other governors out west doesn't seem to be going away. We've tried to have an open dialogue with them, but some people refuse to be reasoned with. How we're going to handle this very volatile and serious situation will be the topic of much discussion. President Woods, as well as President-elect Markovich, will be involved in those conversations.

"In the meantime, something we can all agree on is the new gun control legislation. Both the president and the president-elect understand that this change is challenging for some citizens. The rhetoric from Blackwell and his co-conspirators has caused a lot of anxiety in the hearts of otherwise-peaceable citizens. So, we've decided to declare a one-week amnesty period for folks to turn in their firearms. They can bring those into any state or local law enforcement branch. In areas where there have been some disagreements between local and federal law enforcement, Mr. Szabos is readying his organization to be able to accept those weapons on behalf of a grateful government.

"We also understand some collectors have thousands of dollars tied up in their guns. We will be issuing receipts which can be filed with your taxes for a deduction in the amount of the replacement value of your firearms. Deductions are fully refundable, which means even if you don't owe any tax, you'll get a check for the value of the firearms. It's basically a buyback, it's just that you'll have to wait until tax time to get your money.

"We met with the secretary of transportation, attorney general, and the commerce secretary before coming in. Collectively, we've decided that while citizens have been granted a one-week amnesty for possession, a ban on interstate transport of firearms should go into effect immediately.

"I personally want to urge everyone listening not

to wait until the last minute to turn in your guns. You need to get them together, locate your nearest collection point as long as that does not involve crossing state lines, and get them exchanged for your tax-deductible receipt. No receipts will be issued after the amnesty period, and those in possession of banned firearms will be subject to federal prosecution and up to twenty years in prison per firearm. Thank you all once more for coming out today."

"Mr. Secretary! One quick question. Will you be regulating bows, crossbows, pellet guns, and black-powder weapons?"

The secretary of defense began to walk away but paused. "We said no questions, but that is a very valid inquiry. The answer is not at this time. I'm sure once the inauguration has passed and we're all settled in, we'll revisit that issue. Thanks again." He waved and made a quick exit with the Secretary of Homeland Security.

"Well heck, if it's tax deductible, maybe I'll reconsider." Ava's statement wreaked of sarcasm. She looked to her left and right. Foley and Ulysses wore matching expressions; grim and pensive.

She gave her father several minutes to fume while listening to the sympathetic media personalities praise the wisdom of their dear leader in selecting such prudent men to guide us through this tumultuous period. Ava knew the reporters and their *unbiased* guest commentators would continue to rub salt in Ulysses' wounds as they competed with one another to issue ever finer accolades for the administration. She bided her time, knowing that the pundits were pushing him ever closer to accepting her plan.

# CHAPTER 14

Keep me as the apple of the eye, hide me under the shadow of thy wings, From the wicked that oppress me, from my deadly enemies, who compass me about.

Psalm 17:8-9


The others exited the living room, one by one, eventually leaving only Ava, Foley, and Ulysses by themselves. Ava watched the two of them. Ulysses' ears were a blotchy cranberry color. His eyes glared at the television, and the back of his neck also appeared warm with anger. Foley's arms were crossed and his lips were puckered inward.

Ava felt the two of them would soon have had enough and would likely turn off the television, allowing themselves to calm down and return to their senses. Her scheme required that not to happen. She looked at her father with beseeching eyes. "You know, it's not too late."

Ulysses looked past her to Foley, as if it were up to him to make her give up this unyielding line of petitions.

Foley glanced over only for a moment and quickly turned back to the television. He could have screamed *leave me out of this* and the message would not have been clearer.

Ulysses looked in the opposite direction at the desert landscape picture hanging on the far wall of the living room. But no one was in the far side of the living room nor in the vacant desert painting who could help him plead his case. Turning his head straight, he huffed and clenched his jaw.

Minutes passed and no one spoke.

Ava sat patiently.

Ulysses made a sound somewhere in between a guttural growl and the clearing of one's throat before he spoke. "If I agree to game this out on paper, it by no means implies that I've decided to move forward with the mission. It is an exploratory exercise to investigate the full range of outcomes should we commit to such an endeavor. I'll tell you now, the prognosis is bad; very bad, which translates into being highly unlikely that anything of the sort will ever be executed.

"Do I make myself clear?"

Ava bit her tongue to contain the smile which was about to erupt into a shriek of glee. "Yes, sir."

He leaned over to catch Foley's eye. "Do I make

myself clear?"

Foley seemed amazed to be included in the conversation of which he'd obviously wanted no part. Nevertheless, his answer was straightforward. "Yes, sir."

Early Friday morning, Ava, Ulysses, Foley, and James looked at the computer map of the area where Ava would be making the buy.

Foley fidgeted with the zipper on the front of his black hoodie. "I really wish she wasn't going in there alone."

Ulysses zoomed in on the building where she was to meet Chewy2K. "I've thought this through, and we don't have a choice. This guy is agreeing to meet her because he's a lonely nerd. If one of us goes in with her, we lose the honeypot effect. And I'm not confident enough in Charity's ability to handle herself. If something goes wrong, we'll only have one mission; to get Ava out of there. If Charity is with her, we essentially have two missions.

"If anything happens, we can be inside in a matter of seconds. I'll be on foot, on the side of the building, along Navasota. You guys will be in the truck, parked two blocks up in front of those loft apartments."

"You don't think that looks suspicious? Two guys sitting in a parked car?" James asked.

Ava replied, "Those lofts are almost all young people; lots of low-level drug dealers live in the lofts. People will assume you're waiting for someone inside making a pickup. No one will think anything of it. As long as you're wearing your black hoodies, you'll blend right in."

Foley seemed distressed. "What if they figure out that her phone is transmitting? We may not have time to get her out."

Ava took out her phone. "I'll have a gun, and the only way to figure out the phone is really on is to disable the Void Lock app. I have to draw a very specific design on the screen to make it come on. Until then, the screen is completely black and doesn't respond to the power buttons. It looks like it's turned off."

James crossed his arms. "What if they won't let you bring the phone in at all?"

She said, "That's the only way I can transfer the Monero from my wallet app to theirs unless they just want to trust that I'll send it to them when I get home."

"What's your plan, Ulysses?" Foley inquired. "I'll admit, you make a pretty good homeless person in that outfit, but you don't think some random homeless guy standing on the corner could make these guys nervous?"

"Ava says homeless people frequent the area. Trash cans are lined up along Navasota. I'll pick through them and see if I can find anything interesting. I'll have my rifle in this old Army duffle."

Ulysses turned to Ava. "What's your phrase to call in the troops?"

"I'm going to regret this."

Ulysses nodded. "Any variation of that phrase. You'll regret this, I hope I don't regret this; basically, if you use the word regret, we'll charge in guns blazing. The first sound you hear after you say the word is your cue to get on the floor so you don't get caught in the crossfire."

"Got it, but hopefully everything will go off without a hitch."

"And if they sweep you with a metal detector or frisk you, anything that makes you think they're gonna take your gun, abort the mission. Just walk away. Understood?" Ulysses put his hands on her shoulders.

"Yes." Ava twisted elastic bands around her hair to make ponytails on each side of her head, like the comic book character who Chewy2K would be expecting.

"Playing dress-up for this guy?" Foley frowned.

Ava sighed, surprised that she had to respond to such a comment. "I'm playing dress-up for America. I can't believe you would say something like that."

"I just don't like it. I don't like any of it." Foley looked away from her and glanced at Ulysses, as if to implore him to cancel or modify the plan.

Ulysses was obviously conflicted about the whole thing. He avoided Foley's eyes, picking up his faded duffle bag. "Everyone, make sure your weapons are loaded, magazines are easily accessible, phones are fully charged, and let's roll out."

James asked, "Shouldn't we take time to pray before we leave? I can't imagine a time we've ever needed God's protection more."

"You're right." Foley nodded, dropping his head like he was somewhat ashamed that he'd not been the one to recommend asking for God to bring them home safely.

Ulysses smiled at James. "Why don't you lead us?"

James bowed his head. "Father, I'm afraid. I'm afraid for myself and for Ava. I'm not sure how everyone else here feels, but if they're scared like me, I ask that you'll give us all courage. And I ask that you will hide us from our enemies, watch over us, be our shield. In Jesus' name, I pray. Amen."

Ulysses patted him on the back. "We're all afraid, son. Anyone who says they aren't in a situation like this is either a liar or a lunatic. As long as you don't let it paralyze you, fear will help keep you alive."

The team members made their way to the vehicles. Ulysses rode with Ava in her Jeep. "I switched out your license plate. It's the next best thing to having an unregistered vehicle."

"Where did you get the plate?" She stuck the keys in the ignition and started the engine. "Never mind. I don't want to know."

"I kept the plate off of that Civic, the one those raiders came to the farm in."

Ava looked in the rearview to make sure Foley and James were in Ulysses' truck and ready to follow her. She put the Jeep in gear and drove up the gravel path. Buckley barked as he ran along beside.

"I'll be home soon, Buck. You hold down the fort."

Ulysses stretched out his legs. "Take Ben White Boulevard to I-35. The highways are less risky than the side streets. Drop me off at Medina and 7th. That's five blocks out from the warehouse. You'll have to drive around a while to give me time to get into position, but that'll also reduce your odds of being seen with me in the vehicle by spotters."

"Roger."

"Are you nervous?"

"A little."

He reached over and took her hand. "I'll be watching over you. I'll do everything in my power to make sure you don't get hurt."

"Thanks." She turned to her father. "And thanks for going along with this. I know you didn't want to do it."

"I said I'd support you." He looked in the mirror and rubbed the stubble on his face. Between the lazy eye, the scar on his lower lip running down his chin, his disheveled hair, and raggedy clothes, no one would ever guess that Ulysses was not a bonafide vagrant who dwelt among the warehouses and train tracks which enveloped the area where Ava was to make the buy.

Ava reviewed the plan in her mind as they drove from Paleface to downtown Austin. She exited I-35 and let Ulysses out on the corner he'd requested. She continued up 7th, overshooting the street where the meet was to take place. She watched as Foley maintained a safe distance behind her. She turned right on Chicon and took another right on 5th. Foley pulled to the side of the road at the apartment building two blocks away from where the deal would be made.

Ava made the conference call to Foley and

Ulysses. "Okay, I'm turning off the volume on my speaker and turning on the Void Lock so the phone looks off." Ava made the adjustments and stuck the phone in her pocket. "Foley, blink your lights if you can still hear me."

The lights of the truck behind her turned on and off.

"Dad, tell Foley if you can hear me okay, and have him blink the lights again when you are in position."

Foley's lights flashed once more.

"Okay. Jesus, help us all." Ava pulled up to the blue, dilapidated brick warehouse. It had an entrance door as well as a roll-up garage door. She guessed it had been an auto-repair shop at one point in its life. The neighborhood had been an up-and-coming section of town, popular with young people and artists prior to the turmoil surrounding the election. A high percentage of the population was either directly involved with Antifa and the former SJWL, or at least sympathetic to their cause. Undoubtedly, the new government-sanctioned Social Justice Legion would have multiple outposts in the neighborhood. As such, residents would likely be unmolested by police or National Guard patrols; not that Austin had seen much evidence of either one since Ross had been removed from office and detained.

Ava surveyed the area before getting out of the Jeep. None of the buildings or cars looked like they had been torched in the riots. She suspected this and the surrounding blocks were a sort of Antifa sanctuary. The warehouse across the train tracks from her was in poor repair. It was heavily decorated with graffiti. The bare December trees gave the place more of a desolate feeling than it already possessed. Ava cautiously got out and closed her door. She walked up to the building. The windows were boarded up, so she couldn't see what was going on inside. Paint flaked off the dingy white door, revealing that it had been dark green in a previous life. She knocked.

The sound of the deadbolt clicked through the exterior of the door. It opened and she waited apprehensively. Inside stood a slightly overweight man in his mid-twenties. He had an unkept beard, shoulder-length dark brown hair, and wore a black hoodie, just like Ava's. "Hey, come in."

"Chewy?"

"Yeah, well, Fred." He turned to another man about his age, clean shaven with thick glasses and tight curly hair. "This is Darren."

She made a visual sweep of the premises before walking in. "Nice to meet you."

"And you are?" Darren asked.

"Harley, aren't you expecting me?"

"Yeah, I just thought if we were giving you our real names . . ."

"My friends call me Harley." She nodded to affirm her response. "So, what have you got?"

Fred looked her over and smiled nervously, as if after so many years of playing video games and chatting online in his mother's basement, he wasn't prepared to be talking to a pretty girl in person. He glanced at Darren who looked slightly less intimidated by a real girl. "Um, if we can just settle the matter of the payment, we'll have the goods here in a few minutes."

Ava crossed her arms. "Oh, no! Don't try to pull one on me. You said you had the stuff here."

Fred pecked his fingers from one hand against the other. "It's close. Our supplier doesn't want us having the materials sitting around where we could be robbed. I vouched for you because we've chatted online so many times, but you have to understand, I'd never met you in person."

Ava grunted her displeasure. "Well, I'm not transferring funds until I've seen it."

"How about you transfer half, we'll bring it in, then you transfer the rest?" Darren suggested.

"How about I show you my crypto coin wallet, so you can verify I actually have all the Monero in my wallet, then I'll transfer a quarter of it."

Fred and Darren looked at each other. Fred looked back at Ava and nodded. "I suppose that will be okay."

Ava took out her phone, drew the letters A and F which was her secret code to turn off the Void Lock app and allow her to open her cryptocurrency wallet. "There's my account."

Fred looked on. "That's what we discussed. Here's where to send it." Fred held out his phone for her to see.

Ava made the transaction and reset the Void Lock so Fred and Darren wouldn't see that the phone was on, in case they looked. "You should have it."

Fred checked his screen. "Yep. All set. Let me make a call."

Ava protested. "You know, I didn't want to meet a lot of people."

"Sorry." Fred looked at her sheepishly as he dialed the number. He spoke to the person on the other end. "Yep. It's all good. Come on by."

# CHAPTER 15

My soul followeth hard after thee: thy right hand upholdeth me. But those that seek my soul, to destroy it, shall go into the lower parts of the earth. They shall fall by the sword: they shall be a portion for foxes.

Psalm 63:8-10

Ava waited restlessly, leaning up against an old table and shifting her weight from time to time. "So, you guys live here?"

"Sort of." Fred pointed at the stairs. "We've got a loft over top. But we use the garage for the cause. Meetings, organizing protests, that kind of thing."

"I guess those days are over. We're all legit now." Ava smiled.

Darren laughed. "I know! Sometimes I feel like we're the dog who chases cars. Now we've finally caught one and I'm not sure any of us know what to do with it."

Ava said, "Szabos knows. He'll give us the direction we need."

Fred nodded resolutely. "Yeah, I wasn't too sure how I felt about Markovich, but when I heard he was bringing in Szabos, that put me at ease. In fact, the guy that's coming works directly with the Just Society Foundation."

"Really? Does he know George?" Ava acted impressed.

"He knows the guy directly under him." Darren asserted his knowledge.

A series of three knocks, a pause, then two more knocks came to the door.

"That's them." Fred unlatched the deadbolt.

A thin girl walked in first pushing a dolly with two wooden crates, marked M112, stacked one on top of the other.

Ava looked first at the crates, then at the girl.

"Ava? What are you doing here?"

"Raquel?" Ava's heart began to pound.

The second dolly of explosives wheeled through the door. The man pushing them said, "Oh no! She's not with Antifa!"

Ava looked up to see Chip standing in the doorway. "No! I am. It took me a while to come around, but I'm on board."

"Nope, not buying it." Chip quickly pulled out a thin automatic pistol. "Raquel, lock the door and get your gun out."

Ava shook her head. "I really regret this, the misunderstanding, I mean."

Chip pointed the pistol at her head. "You know, I owe you one from the last time I saw you. Fred, get some tape. Restrain her hands and get her upstairs while I figure out what I'm going to do. Darren, get your gun ready. I'm betting she has people in the area."

Ava's mind raced. They hadn't frisked her and she still had her pistol. But if she drew on them, Chip would gun her down before she got off a single shot.

"Come on, give me your hands." Fred picked up a roll of duct tape and quickly spiraled it around her hands. "Let's go upstairs. You lead."

Ava's pulse pumped like a steam engine. Fear and terror clouded her ability to think. She'd always been able to come up with a solution and be quick on her feet, but this time she felt panic taking over. Ava forced her head to clear enough to make a move. "You and I are going upstairs, and they're staying down there?" She knew it was a stupid question, but it was critical information to Foley, James, and most importantly, her father who were all listening in. With her out of the line of fire, they'd be free to shoot up the lower level.

"Yeah, just keep walking," Fred replied.

Once upstairs, Ava feigned a look of remorse. "Fred, Chip is wrong about me, I don't know why he thinks I'm not with you guys. I don't even care about these stupid explosives. We've gotten know each other for so long online. I really just wanted to meet you, and you're everything I thought you would be. I guess I'm an idiot for thinking this, but I had in my mind that maybe we'd sort of hit it off."

Fred looked into her eyes as she fed him the line. His mouth gaped open, his eyes were mesmerized, he nodded slowly. Fred whispered, "I feel the same way, but let's just get this sorted out with Chip."

"No, Fred! If we're going to be together, we need to get out of here—you and me. Is there a way out?"

Fred looked at the window. "The fire escape."

"Good, get this tape off my hands."

Fred quickly removed the tape and turned to the window to open it.

POW, POW, POW. Gunfire rang out from below. POP, POP, POP.

Fred turned to look at Ava with a curious expression.

BANG! Ava lowered her Glock while Fred's lifeless body slumped to the floor. She crawled over his corpse and out the window.

Ava looked at the alleyway below before pushing down the fire-escape ladder. Seeing no one, she began her descent. Ava hurried down the escape as bullets were flying everywhere on the lower level.

The rear door of the building flew open and Chip ran out, fleeing a hail of gunfire. Ava took aim at him and fired. BANG, BANG, BANG! Chip still held his large pistol as he sprinted past. Ulysses was next out the door.

He paused his pursuit of Chip to check on Ava. "Are you alright?"

"I'm fine. Go! Don't let him get away!" Ava jogged behind Ulysses. They were soon joined by Foley and James.

Chip had a twenty-yard lead and ducked behind the building.

Ulysses put his hand up for the team to slow down. "He could be set up behind that corner to ambush us. Proceed with caution." Ulysses tucked low, took aim at the corner and began to come around.

The sound of wheels of a car screeching to a halt echoed from Chip's direction.

Chip's voice could be heard yelling. "Get out!"

A girl screamed. "Please! Don't kill me! Just take the car!"

Ava followed her father up the street, clearing the corner just in time to catch the tail end of Chip's impromptu car-jacking, and to see him speed off in the stolen silver Kia Soul.

Ava lowered her pistol. The young girl who'd just lost her vehicle looked Ava and the others over and backed away from them. Her pace quickened. She turned and scampered away.

Ulysses looked at Foley and James who were both winded. "You two, go secure the building."

"Got it." Foley nodded and patted James on the shoulder. "Come on."

Ulysses examined Ava's face then her body. "Where's the guy who took you upstairs?"

"By the window." She changed magazines in her pistol. "Dead."

"Lucky him." Ulysses put his left arm around her, keeping his right on his rifle. "I was looking forward to having a conversation with him."

Once Ava and Ulysses reached the inside of the warehouse, Foley called out, "Both males are dead. The girl is bleeding heavily from her right shoulder and left thigh."

"Is she squirting?" Ulysses walked up to Raquel who was lying on the dirty concrete floor.

Foley frisked her before taking out his knife and beginning to cut away the clothing from her shoulder.

Ava stooped beside her. "It doesn't seem to be coming out in spurts, but it's a heavy flow."

Ulysses stood over Raquel. "Best put a tourniquet above the injury anyway."

Raquel moaned in pain. "Ava, don't let me die. Please don't let me die."

"I'm not going to let you die." Ava grabbed the duct tape which Fred had used to secure her hands. She lifted Raquel's bleeding thigh and wrapped the tape over three times. Next, she ran a screwdriver between the tape and Raquel's jeans and turned it to tighten the tape. Finally, she pulled the tape around three more times to secure the screwdriver.

In the meantime, Foley cut the sleeve from Darren's hoodie and used it to make a temporary bandage for Raquel's shoulder.

"My phone is in my right pocket." Raquel seemed to be using all of her strength to lift her head and reach for her phone with her uninjured hand. "Get it and call an ambulance."

Ava pulled the phone out of Raquel's pocket and stowed it away in her own back pocket. "We'll get you some help." She looked up at Ulysses. "We need to take her to Sam. He can get her cleaned up."

Ulysses shook his head and pointed to the back door. "Come outside."

Perturbed, Ava followed him. "She's in bad shape. We need to get her help fast."

Once outside in the alley, Ulysses said, "We can't take her back with us. If we did that, she'd be our prisoner. That means she's sucking up resources that we can't spare. It also means someone has to watch her all hours of the day. We're stretched too thin just trying to keep someone on watch around the clock. We'll call 911 with her phone when we leave. With all the gunshots, police are probably coming already."

"High-priority 911 response times were over an hour before the country melted into chaos. Leaving her and calling 911 is a death sentence."

"She should have thought of that before her and her accomplices lit the fire that melted the country into chaos." Ulysses turned to walk back in. He called out to Foley and James, "We need to get the explosives loaded up. Gather all of their weapons as well. And get all the phones. I want to try to get that Monero back in my account before the screen locks on the phone of the one Ava transferred the funds to. He won't be needing it."

Ava stomped behind her father. "She's my friend, dad. I can't leave her here and hope an ambulance shows up before she bleeds out."

Ulysses stopped short and glared at Ava with harsh eyes. "She's not your friend anymore. You chose to get involved in this war, and now you have to fight the people who are trying to kill you.

"I offered . . . no; I begged you to sit this one out—to help out; support the Alliance from the sidelines. You refused. You wanted to jump in head first. Now you're neck-deep in a civil conflict and you don't get to make up the rules as you go along. The rules of this game were established long before you were born. The rules in this field are kill or be killed. The fact that we are even calling an ambulance, patching her up, giving her any chance of survival whatsoever, goes against every instinct in my body.

"So, we're going to wrap up this operation, and you are going to get on board with the program. If you decided this is too tough for you; good. Tap out and we'll go to Oklahoma. That has always been my first choice."

Ava hated to see Raquel on the ground in such a horrible condition. "Then at least let me put the call in now." She took her phone out of her pocket.

Ulysses snatched it from her hand. "No!" He forcibly retrieved Raquel's phone from Ava's back pocket. "And when it's time to roll out, I'll make the call from her phone. Everyone else on this team understands the chain of command. I've given you way more leeway than I should have because of my guilt. But that ends right here and right now! Fall in line, or you're off the team!"

Ava was instantly perplexed. After all, wasn't it her team? Didn't she get to say who was in and who was out?

Ulysses barked orders at Ava. "Look around and try to locate the detonators. These crates are just the M112 bricks of plastic explosives. All this is for nothing if we can't get detonators."

"Yes, sir." If she ever had been, Ava was no longer in charge. "I never saw them bring in any other boxes. They may still be in their vehicle."

Ulysses softened his face. "Any idea what they may have been driving?"

"Maybe."

"Good, check it out. Foley, watch her back. I'll help James get this other crate loaded into the truck."

Ava led the way out the front door. She saw the familiar blue Maserati parked behind her Jeep. "That's it." She checked the door. "Locked. Maybe Raquel has the keys. I'll be right back."

"Hurry!" Foley kept watch.

She ran inside and rifled through Raquel's pockets. Once she had the keys, she dashed back out to the Maserati and unlocked the door. Ava hit the trunk release and hurried to the boot of the car. "I think we've got 'em."

Foley quickly helped her transfer the crates from the trunk to the bed of the truck then jumped into the cab with James.

Ulysses approached Ava. "Do you want me to drive?"

"I'm fine." She looked at the Maserati. "Foley said you're pretty good at permanently incapacitating a vehicle. Do you think we have time for a quick lesson?"

Ulysses drew his knife with haste, lay down under the car, then popped back up. "Poke the fuel tank on the very bottom. You don't want to hit air and create a spark. That's bad for obvious reasons."

He quickly walked around to all four tires and jabbed the side walls. "Start the Jeep and pick me up." He came back around the first tire and cut a strip out.

Ava got into her vehicle, started the engine, and backed up to Ulysses.

He got in, lit the strip of tire and tossed it into the puddle of gas. "Go!"

Ava sped off while Ulysses dialed 911 on Raquel's phone.

"White female with multiple gunshot wounds at the warehouse on the northeast corner of Navasota and 5th." He removed the back of the phone, pulled the battery and tossed it out the window of the Jeep. Ulysses cracked the phone into two pieces, flinging each fragment in different directions.

"You were right about the plan going wrong. Thanks for getting me out of there." Ava sped south on I-35 with Foley and James close behind.

"You got yourself out. You did good. You're quick on your feet when it comes to solving problems under stress. You did what you had to do with your captor. Anytime you get a chance to get away, take it. And always eliminate anyone who might interfere with your escape."

"Still, if you hadn't been there, I don't think I could have gotten out." She glanced over at Ulysses. "What are you doing?"

"Transferring the Monero back to my crypto-coin wallet."

"So we got all those explosives for free?"

"That was a pretty heavy operation. Back in the day, I called that work. If you think that counts as free, well, I guess we're all entitled to our own opinion." Ulysses closed Fred's phone and pulled the battery out.

"Are you going to get rid of his phone?" Ava asked.

"No. His contacts might come in handy some time. We'll hang on to it."

"What do we do next?"

"Stash these supplies until we find a good place to put them to use."

"When will that be?"

"Easy tiger; slow and steady. Let's get home and celebrate this win before we run off trying to get ourselves killed again."

Ava nodded. She knew the adrenaline would be running out soon, but for now, she was ready to fight!

# CHAPTER 16

Thou art my hiding place; thou shalt preserve me from trouble; thou shalt compass me about with songs of deliverance. Selah.

Psalm 32:7

Ava sat with her legs crossed on the bed of the upstairs apartment over the garage. She didn't get involved in the debate, she simply listened.

James puckered his forehead into deep rows. "Neither one of them saw me. Let me walk the bombs into the collection centers."

"The girl saw you, James. And it's highly likely they've got pictures of all of us up at the firearms collection points," Ulysses argued. "If they do, you'll never walk out alive."

James crossed his arms tightly. "Charity worked with that girl. How do you know Charity won't be one of those pictures?"

"Charity wasn't with us." Foley sat on the bed next to Ava. "She has no reason to think Charity is involved."

"Do I have any say in this?" Charity fumed. "No one has even asked me if I want to do it."

James interrupted, "You don't need to. I'm going to walk it in. So it's an irrelevant discussion."

Ulysses raised his hands for everyone to calm down. After everyone had been given the opportunity to quiet down, he asked, "Charity, how would you feel about walking the bombs into the collection points?"

"I want to do it. I didn't get to go on the last mission. I want to be a part of this."

James began shaking his head.

Ulysses put his hand on James' shoulder. "We'll only send her in if we know they've got too many people turning in weapons for them to check the ammo boxes. The plastic explosives will be buried in the bottom of the ammo cans under boxes of ammo. She'll turn in a gun along with droves of other people anxious to hand over their last morsel of freedom. The clerks set up at the collection point will be in a hurry to get the receipts written and get people out the door. They're liberals, they don't want to work. They just want to go home and watch Oprah."

James growled. "Charity doesn't have to get away with it just once, she has to go to four separate locations. Why are we handing over four guns anyway?"

"For the ruse. It's a small price to pay. Two of them are from the warehouse job anyway. The other two came from the raiders who hit the house. We'll get more guns." Ulysses smiled and nodded. "And if any of the locations aren't busy, we'll skip 'em. Charity will only go to the centers where the workers are likely to be overwhelmed."

Ava sat forward, letting her legs hang off the side of the bed. "So, the plan is to drive around and set off all the bombs as soon as Charity has dropped off the last one?"

"Yes, that's the plan," Ulysses confirmed.

Ava crossed her feet. "We'll kill a couple of the Social Justice Legion processors, and perhaps some of their henchmen who are looting the contraband, but innocent people are going to get hurt."

"Which innocent people?" Ulysses paced to the window and looked out.

"The ones turning in their guns."

"You mean the cowards who are arming the enemy by giving them free guns and ammo?" Ulysses stared down the driveway.

"That's not their intention," Ava defended. "They just want to stay out of it."

"You can't sit on the fence without getting a picket in your tail." Ulysses pivoted back to the group. "We'll be sending two messages. To the enemy; we will not go without a fight. And to the fence riders; peace through neutrality does not exist, so pick a side or have one chosen for you.

"By hitting the collection centers first thing

Monday morning, we may help nudge a few people who are having trouble deciding. The absolute cowards mostly turned in their guns Thursday or Friday. The fair-weather patriots and the people who are conflicted will wait until Tuesday or Wednesday. If they see that capitulation is no more safe than resistance, maybe they'll do the right thing and join in the fight. Even if they decide to bury their guns in the mud, at least the SJL won't have them.

"This is about more than just blowing up a collection point and taking out twenty or thirty Markovich thugs. This is about a violent action against the oppressor and those who support him. It's an event that will energize the patriots, strike fear into the heart of the enemy, and force the uncommitted to lead, follow, or get out of the way."

Charity held James by the arms. "I want to do this. You'll be right outside, and you'll all be listening to what's happening. I'll leave my phone on with the volume all the way down. The same as you guys did with Ava."

James twitched his mouth and looked at Ulysses, as if he blamed him for this cockamamie scheme. "I don't like it." He turned his attention back to Charity. "Promise me that if anything looks suspicious, you'll scrub the plan and come back to the truck."

"I promise." She hugged her new husband tightly. "Come on; help me pick out a couple of rabbits from the hutch. Betty is going to teach me how to make rabbit stew."

James waved as he followed Charity down the

stairs.

"See you in a while," Ava said.

Once the newlyweds were gone, Foley pulled a crate of plastic explosives out from under the bed. "I was thinking, maybe it would be best if we didn't come straight back here after the operation. If we're followed, we'd lead them to Sam's. Not only would that ruin things for him and Betty, it would leave us with nowhere to rendezvous if we get hit and have to split up."

Ava picked up one of the C-4 bricks and inspected it. "What if we took the trailer down to Riemer's Ranch Swimming Hole? It's a public park with a parking lot, but hardly anyone ever goes down there. The park has multiple dirt roads so we could split up if we were to be chased."

"It could work." Ulysses took one of the M112 bricks from the crate and began pressing rows of marbles into the soft outer cover. He secured them onto the brick with duct tape.

Ava watched. "Let's say we head back to the trailer in the park, and we get attacked. If we have to run, and we're able to get away, how long should we wait to go back to the farm?"

"Seventy-two hours." Ulysses secured the ignition component of the detonator to the brick. "So, everyone should have some cash, a pistol, and a pack with food and water. Not much, but some. Too much water will slow you down."

"Which decreases your odds of being around to need it," Foley added.

Ulysses finished adding another layer of marbles to the brick then wrapped it tightly with three more layers of duct tape. "It's a good plan, Ava. Good thinking on your part."

"Thanks." She smiled.

Ulysses handed the improvised explosive device to Foley to inspect. "You, too. Good call on not leading the enemy back to base."

"Thanks." Foley looked over the wad of duct tape and marbles. "This is nice work. I've seen how much damage these little marbles can do once they leave the nest."

"Yeah, unfortunately, this ain't my first rodeo." Ulysses' eyes showed no pleasure in creating the destructive apparatus.

Monday morning, the five-person team sat in Ulysses' trailer which was a mile and a half away from the Hodges' farm, at the public park. When the team left earlier that morning, Sam and Betty had understood something heavy was about to go down, but they'd seemed to know better than to ask questions.

Ulysses pointed to the map saved on his laptop. "The convention center and the library at UT are going to be the biggest collection points. They'll have the highest turnout, the most visibility, and they'll be the most heavily staffed. The two smaller drop-off centers are up north. One is in a strip mall in Windsor Hills. The other is all the way up near Round Rock, in an office park. Those two are extra credit. If anything doesn't look right at those two, we'll walk away in a heartbeat. But the convention center and UT, we need those for this operation to be considered a win."

"The ones up north are a long drive." Ava studied the map.

"About twenty minutes away from the two down south; a straight shot down I-35. We'll split up into two teams. Charity will make the drops up north, then a two-person team will stay there until she makes the drops down south. Once those two devices have been delivered, we'll coordinate the detonations at the convention center and the office park. The two teams will rush to their secondary targets and fire off the other two bombs. Both teams will keep driving in their respective directions and meet in the middle. We'll get off I-35 at Anderson Lane and take that west. It's the scenic route, but that's good. It gives us time to identify any potential tails before coming back here."

"Sounds good. What are the teams?" Charity asked.

"James and Ava will stay up north. Foley and I will escort you south."

"Nope, not gonna happen." James shook his head. "You can't ask me to be split up from my wife. I don't like being in this situation in the first place, but I'm definitely not getting separated from her."

Foley said, "Ulysses and I are the experienced gunfighters. You should trust us to take care of her."

James waved his hands. "I know that's the logical answer, but she's my wife. And that trumps logic. I'm not bending on this one. Rework the teams."

Ulysses looked at James as if he were

contemplating how he was going to respond. Finally, he said, "Okay. I'll take the north side by myself. If something goes wrong up there, I can address it alone. If Charity hits a snag, you'll need all the shooters in one location."

"But all the phones will be connected, and I'll be calling the shots. Once we leave this parking lot, no one argues, no one questions my decisions. Got it?" Ulysses glared at James harshly.

James nodded and looked away.

Ulysses armed the four IEDs and placed them in the bottom of four separate green, metal ammo cans. Next, he covered the devices with boxes of ammunition and clamped the lids shut.

"Foley, grab two of these and follow me out to the vehicles. Ava, grab those four handguns."

They all exited the trailer. Ulysses placed the ammo cans in the floorboard of the Jeep where Charity would be sitting and positioned the corresponding firearm near the box with the matching ammunition. "Keep these pairs matched up. You don't want someone to open the ammo can and wonder why you're handing in .357 ammo with a .22 pistol."

"Yes, sir." Charity got into the passenger's seat of Ava's Jeep.

Ulysses kept two detonator remotes and handed Ava the other two. "They're labeled; convention center and library. When we retreat, we'll take 360 south. When you go over the bridge after the attack, chuck these in the river. But peel the labels off first."

Ulysses stood by as Foley and James climbed

into the rear of the Jeep with their rifles and extra magazines. "Any questions?"

She tucked the detonators in the pockets of her hoodie. "No, sir." Ava started her engine and waited for her father to get into his truck and lead the way.

The one-hour journey to the first collection center went without incident. Ulysses led the way to the office park but pulled into the parking lot of a hotel before arriving. Over the headphones connected to Ava's phone, he said, "I'll wait here."

"Got it." Ava continued to the office park where the collection point was located. She saw several people gathered around a sign with the new red-and-white Social Justice Legion logo. She turned to Charity. "Are you ready?"

"I'm nervous."

James put his hand on her from the back. "Relax. Everyone going in there to turn in guns is feeling nervous. If anything happens, I'll be in there in a second."

Her worried eyes didn't match her smile. "Okay, thanks."

Ava watched as Charity got out of the vehicle, making sure she took the right ammo box for the location and the right pistol to turn in with it. She did.

Ava waited with baited breath as Charity disappeared behind the doors of the collection center. She listened on her headphones. Soon after, Charity's voice could be heard, evidently speaking to another person who'd just turned in their gun. "How long did you have to wait?"

A man's voice said, "Ten minutes. It's moving

pretty fast."

"Thanks," Charity said.

The next ten minutes seemed like an hour to Ava. She felt bad for her friend. Finally, she heard the transaction taking place. The voice of someone Ava assumed was a clerk said, ".22 revolver, Taurus, like new. Here's your receipt. Sorry, you don't get a tax credit for the ammunition, but at least you won't get in trouble for having it."

"Thanks." Charity's reply was brief.

Ava watched the doors. Seconds later, her friend emerged, walking briskly toward the Jeep.

Ava pulled away from the parking spot the moment Charity was back inside the vehicle. "How did it go?"

Charity took a deep breath. "Good, but they have a big picture of your driver's license picture on an 8-inch-by-twelve-inch piece of printer paper. Over top, it says *terrorist*, in big letters. Below it says, *have you seen me? If so call, and it has the telephone number."*

"Dad, did you hear that?" Ava asked.

Ulysses' voice came back. "I got it. They may be looking for your Jeep. Come to the place where I pulled off. We need to switch vehicles. And you should let Foley drive so you can sit in the back. Sink down into the seat when you pull into the collection points."

"Okay." Ava didn't like the idea of her father being in the Jeep, but at least he wouldn't have to drive up to any of the drop-off centers until it was time to detonate the devices.

Ava drove to the hotel parking lot. "You didn't

see pictures of anyone else; James, Foley, or my dad?"

"Just you," Charity answered.

"It was probably Chip who had the posters made up. He's figured out a way to worm his way in with Szabos and parlay his relationship into profits." Ava turned into the parking lot.

"How do you know that guy anyway?" Foley prepared to get out.

Charity was familiar with the seedy details of that answer. Foley was not. Ava wanted to keep it that way. Ava got out of the Jeep. "He's one of Raquel's idiot friends; probably her boyfriend du jour before she got herself all shot up. I'm sure he'll move on to someone with less bullet holes."

"Sounds like a real creep." James quickly transitioned from the Jeep to the back seat of Ulysses' pickup truck.

"How many SJLs were in the collection center?" Foley helped Charity move the ammo cans and pistols to the front seat of the truck.

Charity seemed to be more focused on keeping the weapons near the corresponding ammo cans than on Foley's question. "Um. Six clerks. Maybe four or five guys standing around in the back."

"What did they look like?" Ulysses assisted with the transfer.

"The clerks wore white button-down shirts, all with red ties and red armbands. The guys in the back looked like Antifa thugs who hadn't been issued their new uniforms yet."

Foley asked Ulysses, "Aren't you worried those thugs will get curious about what's in the ammo cans before we get a chance to light them off?"

Ulysses took Ava's keys and handed his to Foley. "It's a possibility. I've tried to lower the odds of that happening by having her turn in that .22 first. Next up is a Kel Tec .32. I'm hoping nobody wants it either. The Smith and Wesson .357 will go to the library then the Beretta 9mm will go to the convention center. That's the one I'm most worried about. But we'll set that bomb off as soon as Charity is back in the truck."

Ava waited for Charity to close her door so she wouldn't hear her next question. "What if one of the bombs is discovered? Don't you think they'll call the other drop-off locations?"

"It's a chance we have to take. Our best option is to keep moving so they have less time to get nosy." With that, Ulysses jumped in the Jeep and started the engine.

Ava frowned at the disconcerting answer, took Foley's AR-15 and got in the back seat of the truck.

Ten minutes later, Foley drove up to the next collection point. Ava saw only one person go in and one come out of the store-front location as Foley pulled up.

"Godspeed!" Ava said as Charity got out of the truck with the second package. She listened while Charity went in and was immediately taken by one of the clerks.

"It's not in the best shape. The IRS will probably only give you about 75% of the replacement value. Here's your receipt."

"That's fine," Charity said. "I'm more concerned with making sure I do the right thing."

"Good attitude. Have a nice day," said the clerk.

Charity was back in the truck less than five minutes after they'd arrived.

"Smooth. You're getting good at this," Foley said.

Charity looked to be on the verge of hyperventilating. "I don't feel so smooth."

James put his hand on her shoulder from the back. "You're doing great. But if you can't handle it, I'll make the last two drops."

Ava wondered if he'd forgotten what Ulysses had said or if James had failed to recall the fact that everyone's phones were on and that her father could hear everything being said in the vehicle. Either way, James would soon remember.

"Absolutely not!" Ulysses' voice yelled over the speaker of Foley's phone. "James, I just finished advising everyone about the chain of command. You'll sit the next mission out. I realize you have no military experience, which is why I'm not kicking you off the team for good."

James huffed.

Foley glanced up at the rearview. "Yes, sir, would be the correct response."

James' voice lacked enthusiasm and held a faint odor of contempt. "Yes, sir."

"I'll be fine." Charity turned toward the back and forced a smile.

Twenty minutes later, Foley pulled onto the University of Austin campus. People were everywhere. National Guardsmen stood arm to arm in a phalanx creating a corridor for a long line of people turning in their firearms. Behind the guardsmen stood a rabble of Antifa soldiers, all carrying black AK-47's and wearing matching black load-bearing vests fully stocked with radios and spare magazines.

A massive crowd made up of members from Right Now wearing home-made riot gear and carrying picket signs protesting the collection centers stood outside the library. Protestors stood behind barricades and chanted. One of the leaders of the protest held a bullhorn. He shouted out, "If you want my gun . . ."

Then the crowd responded, "Come and take it!"

"At least someone is standing up for their rights," James said.

"For now." Foley pointed out several people in plain clothes taking pictures of the protestors. "Once they run those photos against Google and Facebook's facial-recognition program, the Markovich regime will know exactly where to send the SJL henchmen. They'll execute no-knock raids in the middle of the night. These guys will all be disappeared. The time for civil disobedience has expired."

"Look at how long the line is." Charity gazed out the window. "It's pretty chaotic. I wonder how long it will take to get through?"

Ava watched as more and more people entered the line. "I'm not sure. But it is moving."

"Could be over an hour." Charity's voice sounded worried. "What if they discover one of the bombs at another location? They'll know who dropped it off. They could call here and have the National Guard grab me. What will we do if that happens? You guys wouldn't stand a chance in a gunfight against all these soldiers plus the Antifa fighters."

Ava knew every word of Charity's concerns were well-founded, yet she did not want to make things worse. But neither was she willing to lie to her friend in order to quell her fears. She said nothing.

Ulysses' voice came over Foley's speakerphone. "Charity, if you can find a way to make the drop without standing in line, do that. Maybe they have a drop-off desk that doesn't issue receipts."

"Okay. But what if this is the only way?" Charity asked.

"Then it's the only way. I'm sorry," replied Ulysses.

"I understand." Charity dutifully picked up the ammo can and the pistol. She proceeded to fulfill the task she'd signed up for.

James spoke with a grim tone. "If she gets in trouble, I'm going to fight it out. So, if you guys have to leave, let me out first. I'll wait until you're gone to start shooting."

"If she gets in trouble, we'll all fight it out. We're not leaving her behind." Foley watched Charity walk up to the line.

Ava listened to Charity who was speaking to the young guy in line in front of her.

"Do you know if they have a drop-off point where you can just give them the gun? I don't really need the receipt."

"No, but you know the tax credit is refundable, right?"

"Yeah, I know, but I've got to get to work."

"What kind of gun do you have?"

Ava could hear Charity unzip the soft cover gun case.

"Smith and Wesson .357."

"No kidding? That thing is worth some money. At least five hundred. If you don't want the tax credit, do you mind if I turn it in? No sense in letting it go to waste."

"Sure. Can you hand in my bullets also?"

"Yeah, no problem. Thanks."

"No, thank you."

Ava watched from a distance as Charity left the bomb with the unsuspecting guy.

Foley had the truck turned around and ready to exit the parking lot by the time Charity returned. They sped off towards the convention center to make the final drop.

# CHAPTER 17

The wicked plotteth against the just, and gnasheth upon him with his teeth. The Lord shall laugh at him: for he seeth that his day is coming. The wicked have drawn out the sword, and have bent their bow, to cast down the poor and needy, and to slay such as be of upright conversation. Their sword shall enter into their own heart, and their bows shall be broken. A little that a righteous man hath is better than the riches of many wicked. For the arms of the wicked shall be broken: but the Lord upholdeth the righteous. The Lord knoweth the days of the upright: and their inheritance shall be for ever. They shall not be ashamed in the evil time: and in the days of famine they shall be satisfied. But the wicked shall perish, and the enemies of the Lord shall be as the fat of lambs: they shall consume; into smoke shall they consume away.

Psalms 37:12-20

The inside of the vehicle was hushed. Ava watched the doors of the convention center. Far fewer people were attempting to turn in their firearms at the final location.

"I wonder why this collection point is slower than the campus?" Foley gazed suspiciously out the window.

"Free parking at the campus." Ava slumped low in the back seat so not to be seen by anyone walking by the vehicle.

"Wow. I guess that's it," said James.

"I'll take it. I don't think I could stomach standing in line for an hour. I'm ready to get this over with." Charity picked up the last bomb and the pistol which would serve as her final admission ticket into the collection center.

"You'll be fine. It's almost over." Ava tried to instill confidence in her friend, hoping that her words were true.

"And if something goes wrong, you'll be right behind me. Right?"

Ava peeked over the seat to smile at her friend. "With bells on."

"Thanks." With her IED in tow, Charity closed

the door.

Ava said a silent prayer for Charity who was being so brave.

Five minutes later, Charity could be heard speaking with the clerk.

"This is the only gun you own?"

"Yes, sir."

Clank! Ava heard the sound of the ammo can opening.

The voice of another man commented, "9mm ammo. This will come in handy."

"I think it got wet. I'm not sure if it's any good," Charity said. "It's pretty old."

"Looks fine to me," said the second man.

Ava held her breath, hoping the man would not look deeper into the ammo can.

More noise could be heard. "What the heck is this?"

Ulysses' voice came over Foley's speaker. "Get her out of there. Drive up on the sidewalk. Send James inside to get Charity. Ava, you cover James and Charity when they come running out. You have to eliminate anyone who sees the truck. Leave no witnesses. As soon as you're one hundred feet from the building, push the button. I'm going to detonate my targets now."

James was out of the truck and sprinting toward the glass doors before Ulysses finished speaking.

Foley had to back onto the sidewalk from the street corner to get around the metal barricades.

Charity sounded frantic. "It was my uncle's gun and his bullets. He was in the military. I'm not sure what he had in there."

"What's your uncle's name?" asked the clerk.

"I've got to go," she yelped.

Ava rolled down her window and stuck the barrel of the AR-15 out. She flipped the selector switch activating Foley's Tac-Con trigger into rapid-fire mode. She watched James jerk the door open to the convention center. TAT, TAT, TAT, TAT! He squeezed off several rounds inside the door. "Run! Come on!" James continued to fire. TAT, TAT, TAT!

Ava watched the doors of the convention center through her reflex sight. Charity finally appeared.

Foley yelled out the window at Charity. "Jump in the bed of the truck!"

James walked backward, shooting through the glass doors while he retreated.

Charity hopped onto the bumper, over the tailgate, and quickly lay down flat in the bed of the pickup. James followed close behind her.

Two Antifa militants ran out in pursuit of them, AK-47s raised and ready to fire. POW, POW, POP.

Ava returned fire. TA, TA, TA, TA, TA, Ta! Spent brass poured out the window, clanking on the pavement below. "Got one!"

"You gotta get the other one. Remember, no witnesses." Foley punched the gas, shoving Ava against the back seat.

She adjusted herself to regain her stance. She turned off the rapid fire and took steady aim at the remaining Antifa fighter who was leveling his AK-47 toward the truck. POW! The bullet struck him in the chest, and he fell to the ground. Unfortunately, four more men with AK-47s and black vests over black hoodies came pouring out of the doors.

Ava quickly retrieved the detonator from her pocket. She estimated that they were approximately sixty feet from the doors. She hoped the truck was far enough from the explosion. CLICK.

Ava closed her eyes, prayed to God that the device would work and that they'd get away before anyone else saw them. Hearing nothing for what seemed like seconds, she opened her eyes. She wondered if she'd pressed the button of the right detonator.

BOOOOOOM! Fire and glass, and smoke and shrapnel jetted out of the doors, impaling the black-clad aggressors who were taking aim at Ava and her friends.

"What's your status?" Ulysses said over the phone.

"Target one down. No friendly casualties. En route to secondary target." Foley cut the corner hard, slinging Ava against the door.

"Good. My first target is also destroyed."

Ava felt a sense of pride and accomplishment welling up in her stomach, overtaking the feelings of sheer terror and absolute panic induced by the near miss.

Ava watched to make sure they weren't being followed as Foley raced toward the University of Texas campus only miles north of their present location.

"Anything behind us?" Foley asked.

"No. All clear. For now." Ava replaced her magazine with a fresh one. "Should we pull over so Charity and James can get back in the cab? It can't be too comfortable being slung around in the bed of the truck. I'm sure it's bumpy, also."

"We can't stop for that. We're up against the clock." Foley glanced at the rearview. "The truck bed is more comfortable than a bullet."

James spoke over the mic on his earphones. "We'll be okay back here. Do what you've gotta do."

When they arrived at the campus, people were running in every direction. The National Guard had positioned heavily armored vehicles by the front doors of the library and appeared to be evacuating the building.

"I guess they know they're under attack." Ava held the second detonator in her hand.

"We can't get any closer than this without somebody seeing that we have a guy with a rifle lying in the bed of our truck." Foley slowed as they drove by.

"Should I hit it now?" Ava asked.

"I'm going to get the truck turned around so we'll be headed toward the I-35 on-ramp. But be ready."

"Okay." Ava held the detonator firmly in her sweaty hands.

Foley pulled into a parking lot to turn around. He drove at a moderate pace back toward the library. "We have to hope this is close enough. Get ready."

"Finger is on the button," Ava took a deep breath and held it.

"Go!"

Click.

KABOOOOOM!

Fire, ash, smoke, and debris exploded like a volcano from behind the two military vehicles parked in front of the library's front doors.

"Hang on back there!" Foley pulled up onto the sidewalk to drive around the car in front of him that had stopped to see what happened.

"Got it!" James' voice came through the phone.

Ava looked through the back window to see Charity and James being jostled around the back of the truck by the rough ride.

An older model gold car coming from the opposite direction had three passengers in black hoodies with Antifa armbands. The girl in the front passenger's side and the man in the rear noticed the truck and yelled for the driver to give chase.

"They made us." Ava shoved the detonator back in her pocket and readied her rifle.

"What's your status?" Ulysses asked over the phone.

"Target is detonated, but we've got a car full of hostiles in pursuit," Foley replied.

"What are they doing?" Ulysses asked for clarification.

"They want me to pull over."

"Do it. As soon as they get out of the car, have James pop up from the bed of the truck and light them up. Ava, you be ready, also," her father said.

"Let me know when to start shooting," said James over the phone. "I've got a fresh magazine and my finger is on the trigger."

"Roger that." Foley drove under the overpass and pulled to the side. He rolled his window down. "Are you guys okay?"

The driver jumped out of the car with a semi-automatic pistol in his hand. "We're fine, but we noticed you trying awfully hard to get away from the scene."

The two passengers also stepped out of the vehicle. The male was armed with an AK. The girl held a shotgun with a pistol grip.

Foley acted surprised. "Of course! Didn't you guys see that explosion? I wanted to get out of there, in case there was another blast."

Ava sunk low in her seat and watched the leader approach the truck through the side view mirror.

"Step out of the car," said the man with the pistol.

"Hit it, James," Foley yelled.

Ava stuck her rifle out the window and began shooting in tandem with James. They cut down the two men before they knew what had hit them.

BOOM! The girl's riot gun blasted. Ava saw multiple spiderweb cracks appear on the back windshield of the truck. She watched James take a hit from the shotgun. He was knocked flat against the bed of the truck.

Charity screamed, "James!"

Ava lined up the red reticle of her reflex sight with the girl's chest. She watched the girl pump another shell into the chamber. Ava squeezed the trigger. POW!

The girl dropped the shotgun and fell to the ground.

"Go! Go! Go!" Ava shouted.

Foley gunned the engine and sped toward the on-ramp.

"Status?" Ulysses asked.

Ava turned around to look through the cracked glass of the rear windshield. "James was hit with a shotgun. He's bleeding from his face, neck, and shoulder. Can you hear me, James?"

"Yeah," A mumbled and weak voice replied.

"How are you doing? Can you see out of both eyes?"

"Yeah, I can see. But I've got a lot of blood coming out of my face. I've got a pellet in my cheek and my jaw."

Ulysses said, "You can see and you're conscious. That means it could be worse. You'll be home in no time. Sam will get you fixed up."

Ava asked her father, "Did everything go okay on your end?"

"Yes, I'm about five minutes out from Anderson Lane."

"Us, too," Foley added.

James' injury added to the tension for the ride home and put a dark cloud over the glory of their achievement.

When they had to stop at the first red light on Bee Cave Road, Ava rolled down her window and tossed the first aid kit to Charity. "Keep pressure on the wounds. We're almost home."

Foley spoke into his phone. "Ulysses, are you confident enough that we aren't being tailed to go to Sam's? Or would you prefer to have Sam meet us at the trailer?"

"I've stayed ten-cars back from you since you got on Anderson. I haven't seen anyone tailing you. If anyone is being followed, it would be me. I'll go back to the trailer. You get James to Sam's. He'll be much better equipped to deal with his injuries at the house rather than trying to haul all of his supplies out to the trailer.

"But regardless of whether or not I'm being tailed, this Jeep belongs to Ava and we know they're looking for her. We're going to have to get rid of it. And Ava, pull the battery out of your phone, in case they're tracking your GPS."

"Okay. Foley's phone is on speaker, so I'll still be able to hear you." Ava had another twenty minutes of having to watch her friend's distress through the shattered glass as Charity tried to control the bleeding of her husband in the bed of an old pickup truck.

# CHAPTER 18

The wicked borroweth, and payeth not
again: but the righteous sheweth mercy, and
giveth.

Psalms 37:21

Dressed and ready to go, Ava sat on the wooden
stairs of the weathered front porch Tuesday
morning. She gently ran her fingers through
Buckley's fur. The dog flopped his bushy tail every
few seconds as a sign that she was in the right spot.
Directly behind Ava, Foley cleaned his rifle in the
swing, which was suspended from the roof of the
covered porch by a galvanized metal chain on either
side.

Still in her robe, Charity walked out the door of
the well-kept farmhouse with a cup of coffee and

took a seat next to Ava on the stairs.

"How's James?" Ava asked.

"Still sleeping. Sam said it's best if he stays sedated for a couple of days. He pulled eleven pellets out of James' face, neck, and shoulder. He gave him antibiotics, so Sam thinks the risk of infection is low, as long as we keep his wounds clean. It could have been a lot worse."

Foley applied a few drops of oil to the barrel of his gun and wiped it with an old tee-shirt. "At that range, a larger shot size probably would have been fatal. It's a good thing for James that Antifa doesn't know #6 shot is more effective on squirrels than people. If he'd taken buckshot in the face and neck, today would be a sad day."

Charity listened then turned back to Ava. "Believe me, I've gone over that a thousand times in my mind since yesterday. I don't know what I'd do if I lost him."

Ava pulled her close. "You did good. You're a tough cookie. I'm proud of you."

"Thanks." Charity's head hung low. "But I'm not sure I'm cut out for all of this. From the time we left the trailer yesterday, I had this feeling that I'd bitten off more than I can chew. And with each successive drop-off point, I got more and more anxious. By the time that clerk opened up the ammo can to look inside, I was already a complete train wreck. And then James coming in shooting, I thought I was going to pass out right then and there."

"But you didn't." Ava hugged her. "You soldiered on. You got through it and completed your mission. All the fear that you felt, that doesn't matter. You did what you had to do anyway, and that's what makes you a hero."

"I don't feel like a hero." Charity looked off into the distance. "The news is calling us terrorists."

"Yeah, that's what they called our founding fathers." Ava kept one hand on Charity's shoulder and with the other, she resumed petting Buckley.

Foley stuck the magazine in his freshly oiled rifle and closed the charging handle. "One man's terrorist is another man's freedom fighter."

Charity sighed. "I don't care what the liberal media calls me. But I dreamed about that guy I gave the ammo can to at the library. I dreamed he was still holding it when you blew up the device. I mean if we're killing civilians, we're as bad as they say."

"Supplying weapons to the enemy is considered treason. The legitimate government in the Alliance States doesn't consider anyone at any of the amnesty collection points to be innocent civilians. And treason carries the death penalty." Foley began to disassemble James' rifle for cleaning. "If Governor Blackwell were here, I'm sure he'd award you with a medal for bravery. What you did will go down in the history books."

"Thanks." Charity glanced back at Foley. "But I'm not sure I can do anything like that again."

Ava said, "We're all pretty shaken up from yesterday. Dad wants us to lay low for a while. So, rest, take it easy, and we'll talk about it after you and James have had a chance to recover. It would be a shame to lose you as part of the team. Because, like Foley said, what you did deserves a medal.

Very few people could have pulled that off as coolly as you did."

Ulysses pulled up the driveway, with his trailer in tow. He drove around the house, positioning the travel trailer on the back side of the house. Afterward, he walked around to the porch. He wore a short-sleeved plaid shirt and his typical blue jeans over his black leather combat boots. Being concealed by the jeans, the boots looked like an average pair of work shoes. His suppressed short-barreled rifle was slung over his back and a tan tactical sling over his shoulder. "I was listening to the radio on the way back. Collection points in Florida, Arkansas, and West Virginia were attacked this morning. The news is calling them copy-cat terrorists. I call them patriots.

Ulysses pointed at Ava, Charity, and Foley. "But you folks inspired them to take action. Sometimes it just takes a few people to stand up and do the right thing. Then the idea catches on."

Ava patted Charity who was beginning to smile after Ulysses' accolade. "See! You did good."

"So did you." Ulysses looked lovingly at his daughter. "You ready?"

"Yeah." Ava stood to her feet.

Buckley whined at the cessation of his attentive scratching session.

"Is it okay if Buck comes along?" she asked.

"He's earned a lot more than a ride in the truck for his faithful duties as chief sentinel. I suppose it's the least we could do." Ulysses bent down. "Charity, you're on watch. If Buckley rides with us, you'll have to be twice as alert."

"You can count on me for that." She took a swig of her coffee and got up from the porch. "I'll be dressed and in the FROG with my rifle before you guys get out of the drive."

"Keep your battery out of your phone unless you have trouble. Since we know they're looking for Ava, we have to assume all our phones are compromised. I'll power mine up once we're ten miles out. We'll see if we can scrounge up some burner phones while we're in Taylor."

"We're going all the way to Taylor just to ditch my Jeep?" Ava called Buckley to follow her.

"Yeah, it's in the opposite direction from Austin. When the SJL finds it, hopefully, it will throw them off of our trail. But at the very least, it won't provide any clues about which way we went when we evacuated the city."

"Be safe." Charity opened the front door.

"Tell Sam and Betty that we're leaving. And let them know Buckley is coming with us." Ulysses adjusted the strap of his rifle. "Foley, can you come?"

"Yes, sir." He quickly reassembled James' rifle in a few short steps. "I just need to grab a few magazines."

"Take your time. Would you mind driving? My truck is obviously on the most-wanted list after yesterday."

"No problem at all."

"Good. I've got a fresh license plate for you. I'll have it on by the time you get your magazines." Ulysses retrieved a screwdriver and an auto tag from his tactical bag. "Ava, you ride with Foley in his truck. I'll drive your Jeep. Since Markovich's henchmen are looking for you and the vehicle, it will help to not have you in it."

"Thanks. Is it okay for me to power up my phone when we're ten miles out? I'd like to see if I've received any texts."

Ulysses knelt by Foley's back bumper and made a hasty exchange of the two tags. "No. They'll be watching for a signal from your phone. The least little movement could tip them off." Ulysses took Foley's original license plate and tucked it under his seat. He closed the door of the truck. "On second thought, why don't you wait until we get to Taylor. You can power it up and check your messages there. It will add to the pretense that you're operating out of that area."

"Fantastic, thanks," she said enthusiastically. "Come on, Buck. Get in." Ava held the back door open for the dog who seemed thrilled about going for a ride.

Foley came out with his AR-15, Ava's rifle, and a backpack full of magazines. "Ready when you are."

Ulysses handed him a walkie-talkie from his side bag. "We should stay close enough for these to work. Leave a few car lengths behind me and only break radio silence if you see signs of trouble."

"Roger that." Foley passed Ava her rifle, tossed his pack in the center of the cab, turned on the radio, got in, and closed the door.

Ulysses led them far out of the way to avoid driving up I-35 and passing through Austin. The route which traveled through Marble Falls and

Burnet took more than two hours, but greatly reduced the odds of them hitting any license plate readers.

The first stop was to drop the Jeep in a warehouse parking lot near the train tracks in the center of Taylor, Texas. Ulysses removed the plates and replaced them with Ava's official plates, hoping that the vehicle would be found and identified by the SJL. He got in the truck with Foley, Ava, and Buckley. "Okay, let's hit the Walmart. I'll pick up some prepaid phones for everyone. You two stay in the vehicle."

"Can I check my messages while we're waiting?"

"No. We don't want your phone to ping anywhere near there. They could come looking for pre-paid phones sold from that location. After I'm finished at Walmart, we'll drive to the other side of town. You can check your messages there then we'll head home."

"Okay," Ava said.

Foley drove four miles to the Taylor Walmart. Four men armed with crossbows and black powder guns stood guard out front. "Who do you think they're working for?"

Ulysses peered carefully out the window. "I'm not sure. I doubt Walmart would hire armed private security. My guess is that they're local volunteers who are there so Walmart will stay open. I'm sure Taylor has had their share of harassment from the unofficially sanctioned gangs who have been tasked with harassing small conservative towns."

"If MS-13 or Tango Blast shows up, those

weapons won't be much of a deterrent." Ava examined the watchmen.

Ulysses nodded. "Since the ban was issued, they can't get away with standing out front with battle rifles. Although, that doesn't mean they don't have some stashed nearby, in case of an encounter."

He exited the truck. "Sit tight. I'll be right back."

"And if you're not?" Ava asked.

"I'll be fine. If I see trouble then I'll turn around and run. Drive towards me. I'll jump in the bed of the truck." Ulysses shut the door and started toward the store.

Ava watched nervously while Ulysses walked toward the store.

Fifteen minutes later, Ulysses walked out the door with a shopping bag in his hand.

Foley had the engine started and the truck in gear ready to roll as soon as Ulysses closed his door. "Did you get any info on who those watchmen are with?"

"Didn't ask." Ulysses pointed over the back seat. "Drive to the east side of town. Ava can check her phone then we'll head home."

Foley turned in the direction Ulysses indicated. "I was just thinking, if those guys are that organized and disciplined to keep their town up and running, they might be good people to know."

"Maybe, maybe not." Ulysses sat back in his seat. "For the types of operations we're pulling off, we don't need any help. They can do their thing and we'll do ours. Unless you have a centralized command structure, the more people you get involved with, the more complicated it gets."

"Yes, sir." Foley continued to the east side of town.

Buckley hung his head out the window and let the wind flap his tongue against his face. Ava reached around to pat his side. "Enjoy it while it lasts, buddy. It's getting chilly, and I'm going to have to roll up that window."

"Pull over here," said Ulysses. "Ava, check your phone and let us know when you're done."

"Thanks." She replaced the battery and the back cover. Ava powered on her phone and waited for the screen.

"Yep. I've got a text from the girl who lived downstairs from me, Megan. It says she and her little girl are fine. Her family moved to Wyoming before the gun ban. Not coming back until this is all over."

Ulysses put his hand on her shoulder. "Don't text her back."

"Why not? She's in the Alliance States. Markovich can't do anything to her."

"Don't be so sure about that. The same way we're operating in enemy territory, he has agents who are doing the same thing. If the SJL thought they could get information on you, they wouldn't hesitate to snatch up your friend . . . or her little girl."

"Oh. I didn't think of that." The corners of Ava's mouth dropped. "I got a text from Raquel. It came last night. She says Chip knows I was involved in the bombings."

"That's not a surprise." Foley looked around as if scanning for potential threats. "Considering that we used his explosives. But I thought we dumped her phone on the side of the road."

"I guess she got a new one with the same number. Anyways, it says Chip's going to hunt me down and kill me unless I turn myself in. She's claiming that Chip has been given command of a group of SJL fighters specifically tasked with finding me and my accomplices."

"What else does it say?" Foley inquired.

Her pulse quickened as she continued reading the text. "Raquel says if I turn myself in, I'll be prosecuted, but they'll take the death penalty off the table. She also says they'll leave the rest of you alone." Ava looked up at Foley then turned to her father.

She considered the offer in the back of her mind, imagining for a moment that the two men she loved could be spared the wrath of the dictatorial regime.

"That's an absolute lie," Ulysses said. "If you turn yourself in, they'll torture you until you've given up the names and locations of everyone else involved, then they'll leave you on a cold concrete floor to die a slow death. I've worked with communists. I know how they operate. They never keep their end of the bargain, and they never tell the truth."

"Anything else?" Foley quizzed.

"She says to consider this fair warning." Ava growled in frustration and disgust. "I guess I should have killed her at the warehouse."

Ulysses gripped her shoulder. "You're merciful. That's a good trait. Don't let war purge that out of you. Do what you have to do when you have to do it. But if you don't have to, don't.

"Tactically, maybe it was a mistake. But you'd have had a hard time living with yourself if you'd killed her when she posed no immediate threat. It would have cost you your humanity. If you lose that, you've lost everything. We can be tough; brutal even. But we have to be able to see the fine line that makes us inhumane; un-human."

Ava considered his words and gazed at her phone.

"Anything else?" Foley asked.

"No." She pulled the back plate off her phone and removed the battery.

"Let's go home, Foley." Ulysses leaned back in his seat.

Minutes later, they were outside of Taylor and on their way home. Foley glanced over at Ava. "I don't want any details, but just tell me something."

"What?"

"This guy, Chip, he seems to have it out for you, like it's not just business, but personal."

Ava sighed. She hid this nasty little secret as long as she could. "There's not many details to give. Raquel sorta set us up once. He tried to put the moves on me. I said no. He got a little too aggressive, so I had to give him a good kick between the legs."

"That explains it." Foley looked up at Ulysses in the rearview. "I think this guy is going to be a constant thorn in our side. Would you consider organizing a preemptive strike?"

Ulysses replied, "I would. You're right; he's going to be a problem. Ava, do you know where he might be living?"

She really didn't want to admit that she'd been to his house, but she couldn't lie. "Yes. If he hasn't moved."

"We need him alive," Ulysses said. "He's got information. He knows things that we can pass on to Blackwell and the Alliance."

"He's not going to volunteer that info, sir." Foley's nostrils flared.

"Well, try not to enjoy getting it out of him too much," said Ulysses.

"Of course not, sir." Foley fought a grin.

Ava couldn't help but be a little flattered. Neither could she help feeling no remorse for anything that Chip might have to endure.

# CHAPTER 19

When a strong man, fully armed, guards his own palace, his goods are in peace. But when a stronger than he comes upon him and overcomes him, he takes from him all his armor in which he trusted, and divides his spoils. He who is not with Me is against Me, and he who does not gather with Me scatters.

Luke 11:21-23

Ava walked into the kitchen at daybreak Wednesday, loaded the coffee maker, and turned it on. Nothing happened. "Huh. Must have tripped the breaker." She pressed the reset button between the outlets. Still, the machine did not power on. Ava flipped the lights, but likewise, they failed to come on.

Sam Hodge came into the room. "Power is out."

"Oh? What happened?"

"I'm not sure. I called the power company, but I keep getting an *all lines are busy* message. Your dad ran an extension cord from the trailer into the house so he could power the WiFi router. Hopefully, we'll know something soon."

Ava heard Foley coming down the stairs. He entered the kitchen carrying a hand-held radio. "Good morning."

Ava gave him a hug. "Not without my coffee, it isn't."

"We'll boil some water on the grill and get you taken care of." Foley turned to Sam. "I found my radio. I scrolled through the stations, but no one is talking about a power outage. Maybe it's just this area."

Betty walked into the kitchen. "Y'all don't fret. I'll make us some eggs, pancakes, and country ham out on the gas grill."

Ulysses entered, opened his laptop and took a seat at the bar. He clicked away at the keyboard and waited.

"What's happening?" Ava asked.

"According to the power company, the grid is strained, so they are prioritizing electricity to critical areas."

Ava pressed her lips together. "It was 45 degrees last night and supposed to be in the mid-60s today. December in central Texas is the time of year that we use the least power. Something doesn't sound right."

Ulysses punched away on the keyboard again. "That's the official story. I'm guessing the liberal population centers, Houston, Dallas, Austin, and San Antonio are all getting prioritized. And all the small towns are in the dark."

"So, do you think the administration is behind this?" Sam inquired.

"Without a doubt." Ulysses focused on the screen.

Betty gathered her ingredients to take out on the deck to cook. "But why? If Markovich is trying to win hearts and minds, this is a bad way to go about it. He's just pushing everyone in the small towns into the arms of the Alliance States."

"Look what we're having to do to get information." Ava gestured toward her father's computer. "No power means no internet, unless people have an alternate way of keeping their router plugged in. This means they don't have to shut down the web. Antifa and the SJL still have power and internet. But us country folk get neither. If organizations like Oath Keepers and Right Now can't communicate, then Markovich doesn't have to worry about them resisting."

Foley stood behind Ava with his arms around her waist. "Oath Keepers are better positioned for this than Right Now. Most of them either have Ham radio capabilities or someone in their group does. Right Now is mostly young people dependent on cell phones and internet for communication."

Sam looked at his phone. "I still have phone service."

"Yeah, but without a way to charge your phone, you wouldn't for long." Ava held Foley's strong hands with her own.

"Most people have a phone charger for their cars." Betty picked up the eggs and pancake mix.

Ava broke free from the warmth of Foley's arms to help Betty carry some pans to the deck. "Still, it's a hassle. If people have to worry about not having electricity, they'll be too consumed with coming up with workarounds to bother pushing back against the regime."

Foley also assisted with packing the supplies out to the grill. "I'll have to hand it to Markovich, it was a good tactic. But it makes me wonder, what will be the next shoe to drop."

James and Charity joined Ava and the others for breakfast at the Hodges' big dining room table. Foley prayed to bless the meal then everyone began eating.

Ava asked, "Dad, did you find any more information related to the power outage?"

He nodded as he spooned a healthy portion of scrambled eggs onto his plate. "It's widespread. Just as we suspected, the cities are largely unaffected; even out into the suburbs. While most every small town and the majority of rural areas in Texas are blacked out.

"But I found some information that is even more interesting than that." He forked three pancakes onto his plate and passed the platter to Ava.

"Oh?" Sam Hodge cut into a thick slice of country ham on his plate.

"Woods or Markovich, depending on how you want to look at it, has purged all top-level generals who have been less than exuberant about their support for Markovich." Ulysses took a bite of his pancakes.

"That's not surprising. We haven't heard anything about it on the news." Foley handed the syrup to James, who still looked drowsy.

Ulysses finished chewing. "Another event you won't hear about on the news is that the regime sent two battalions of Marines from Camp Pendleton to secure the Dugway Army Base in Utah."

"Really? I've never even heard of that base. I figured if Markovich was going to risk firing the first shot he would've invaded Minot, North Dakota. That's where all nukes are; at least the ones in the Alliance States." Ava cut another bite of pancakes.

Ulysses elaborated, "Dugway is the chemical and biological weapons storage and research facility. Other than small precision tactical nukes, neither side would consider using nuclear weapons. When your enemy is as geographically integrated as the Markovich regime and the Alliance States, mutually assured destruction takes on a whole new meaning.

"I expect we'll see a very intense war between the states. We'll witness conventional and asymmetric aspects, but I don't think it will go nuclear."

"What happened with the Marines? At Dugway?" Sam inquired.

"Oh, they secured the base alright." Ulysses smirked as he cut his pancakes. "Right after they defected and pledged support to Blackwell and the Alliance States."

The table erupted into cheers and applause.

Ulysses waited for the noise to settle. "A similar incident occurred yesterday that didn't make the news; at least not the news we're fed. Woods sent one of his new generals to Boise on Air Force Two. I guess he was going to attempt to intimidate Blackwell, which will never happen. Eight F-35s flew alongside as an escort. All the pilots and Marines working as the general's security detail defected. The general is being held, and supposedly Blackwell is offering to exchange him for President Ross."

"That's awesome!" Ava exclaimed. "What's the name of that darknet message board where you're getting all of this information?"

Ulysses hesitated before answering, as if he were considering how much trouble Ava could get in, should he reveal his source. "It's called Black Ops, but you're not getting my login credentials."

"That's fair," Ava said sheepishly.

Foley sipped his coffee. "Eight F-35s. At a hundred million each, that adds up quickly."

Ulysses grinned. "I doubt Markovich will be sending additional highly-trained service personnel into the Alliance States. He's afraid of losing what's left of his grip on the US military."

"So, he's taking it out on us, by turning our lights out." Charity shook her head. "How childish."

After breakfast, Ava helped Sam feed the animals. "You caught another hog last night?"

Sam poured the slop over the fence into a bucket he'd cut down the center to make a homemade trough. "Yep, a boar. He'll round out the collection very nicely. But now we've got three pigs to feed. We'll have to get some more winter vegetables going so we have enough left over to keep them fed." Sam pointed at one of the rows in the garden. "That's all sweet potatoes. The little ones are a hassle to peel. We can give those to the hogs. They get the pea pods, and we'll never eat all of that cabbage. Still, I don't want to be cutting it close. Once those sows get pregnant, they'll eat a lot more."

"We're blessed to be in Texas. Could you imagine how difficult it would be to grow food for animals up north if you hadn't planned on it?" Ava watched the hogs devour the small pail of scraps.

"It would be rough. Come on, let's scrounge up some greens for the rabbits and chickens." Sam led the way.

"Ava," Foley called out.

She turned around quickly to see him jogging toward her. "Is everything okay?"

"Yeah, but I think we just figured out what Markovich is up to."

"What's up?"

"I just heard it over the radio. He's sending Woods to NRG Stadium."

"Sending the president to Houston at the onset of a full-blown civil war?" Sam held his empty pail behind his back. "Markovich has to know he'll be a target for the more militant elements of Right Now. No other state in the union is as evenly divided as

Texas."

Ava contested the claim. "Maybe Washington State, but they're not living next door to one another. The liberals are on the coast and the patriots backing the Alliance States are all inland."

Foley said, "If Woods is shot in Houston, he'll be a martyr. And it won't be any skin off of Markovich's back. But I think you're right, Sam. He'll be a target."

"Any idea why he'd agree to this?" Ava inquired.

"You mean besides being Markovich's puppet? People in Ulysses' message board are claiming it's going to be a giant recruitment rally to persuade Antifa and the gangs to join the military. The regime wants fresh blood amongst the ranks. They need people that they don't have to worry about defecting or going AWOL. It's kind of embarrassing when you invade a hostile territory and half of your troops walk off the battlefield. Markovich needs people who are loyal to the revolution."

Ava sighed. "We can't let that happen. We have to think up a way to throw a wrench in the plan."

"Ignorance is bliss they always say. Since I'm not going to be involved, the less I know the better. I'll leave the two of you to your scheming." Sam waved and took his pail to the garden.

Foley watched quietly until Sam Hodge was out of earshot. "The rally is this Sunday. We'll have to put our mission to capture Chip on hold."

"He's not going anywhere. Any ideas on how to disrupt Woods' call to arms?"

"No. Secret Service will be all over the place. Whatever we do, it will have to be a peripheral attack, something outside of the actual event. But Secret Service will already be skittish about the whole thing. The least little disturbance will trigger their evacuation protocols and they'll get Woods out of the city, making the rally a non-event." Foley turned to go back toward the house. "Let's go talk it over with your dad."

Ava looked at the garden. "I told Sam I'd help him with feeding the animals. Tell Dad I'll be there in a little while." She kissed him on the lips and returned to her task.

## CHAPTER 20

To every thing there is a season, and a time to every purpose under the heaven: A time to be born, and a time to die; a time to plant, and a time to pluck up that which is planted; A time to kill, and a time to heal; a time to break down, and a time to build up; A time to weep, and a time to laugh; a time to mourn, and a time to dance; A time to cast away stones, and a time to gather stones together; a time to embrace, and a time to refrain from embracing; A time to get, and a time to lose; a time to keep, and a time to cast away; A time to rend, and a time to sew; a time to keep silence, and a time to speak; A time to love, and a time to hate; a time of war, and a time of peace.

# Ecclesiastes 3:1-8

Ava took a seat next to Foley at the small dining table inside her father's travel trailer. "What did I miss?"

Ulysses turned his laptop sideways and pushed the back of it against the window of the trailer. He pointed to the map of the area around the stadium. "We have limited options. NRG Stadium, itself, is fairly isolated. It's completely surrounded by parking lots or other buildings in the complex. The old Astrodome sits directly across from it. No doubt, it will be crawling with security, so it's out as a place from which to launch an attack. Same thing with the convention center.

"Anything we do is going to be small potatoes, so we'll have to execute a multi-pronged assault. Multiple minor strikes could add up to a lot of confusion amongst the security coordinators and still accomplish the objective we're hoping to achieve.

"I expect to see protestors and supporters demonstrating on the greenways at all four corners of the stadium. This strip mall is about a quarter mile to the north. We could possibly initiate an attack via drone from the parking lot."

"How would you attack with a drone?" Ava inspected the map.

"We could attach a brick of plastic explosives and set it down right on top of the stadium. I checked the forecast for Sunday, sunny and low sixties, but I still expect they'll have the roof closed for Woods' visit. If not, then we can drop the charge right inside. Either way, an explosion anywhere near the stadium will warrant an evacuation of the president, and that will be the end of the rally."

"So that's all we need to do." Ava looked up at her father.

Ulysses shook his head. "No. Too small. We need to cause a grand commotion. Something too big for the mockingbird media to sweep under the rug."

"What else do you propose?" Foley asked.

Ulysses pointed at a hotel on the map. "This place is half a mile to the south. It's nine stories tall, so a sniper on the roof could cause some real trouble with a decent scope. If you had Markovich supporters demonstrating on the southeast or the southwest corner, they would provide a target- rich environment for the shooter."

Foley nodded.

"Wait a minute!" Ava objected. "Are you guys serious? You're talking about shooting into a crowd of demonstrators." She turned to Foley. "And you're okay with this?"

"Ava." Ulysses reached across the table to take her hand, but she pulled away. "This is war. You chose this path—for all three of us." Ulysses glanced at Foley. "Or at least for yourself and for me. Though I expect Foley has seen his share of bloodshed and could have been persuaded to lend support from the background; or at least had the good sense to fight from behind friendly lines.

"But remember, these are the same people who

tried to kill you when you went to vote back in November. If I hadn't been there, I doubt you'd be breathing today.

"Beating down anyone in Texas or Florida who dared to vote for Ross is how they stole the election from the American people. We're not talking about shooting a random bunch of innocent people with political leanings different from our own. These are treasonous traitors, violent people, who will stop at nothing to wrestle America away from its rightful heirs and bring about a communist revolution.

"These are the soldiers Markovich hopes to recruit into his new military guard; these are the fighters who will be invading the Alliance States in the months to come. If we don't kill them now, we will have to fight them later."

She listened to her father's reasoning, but she couldn't make it right in her head. "No. We're sneaking up on people. You told me not to sacrifice my humanity, that winning the war doesn't matter if I lose who I am."

A knock came to the door then it swung open. "Hey, guys. What's up?" Charity stepped up into the trailer.

Ulysses answered, "We're having a discussion. Ava told me that you aren't sure about being involved in future actions."

Charity glanced down at the toes of her tennis shoes. "Um, I don't know. When are you planning to go back out?"

"This weekend," said Foley.

Charity looked at Ava with concern. "So soon? James hasn't even healed up. He's in no shape for another mission."

Ulysses nodded. "No problem at all. Why don't the two of you sit this one out; help Sam and Betty hold down the fort. Take your time, let James get better, and you figure out if you're up for another mission. This war isn't going to be over anytime soon. You'll have plenty of opportunities."

"Are you sure?" Charity toyed with the zipper of her jacket.

"I'm positive." Ulysses gave an affirming nod.

"Thanks." A look of relief came over Charity's face.

Ulysses stared at her standing in the doorway for a few moments then said, "But if you're not coming, it's better for everybody if you don't know the details of the mission."

"Oh! Right. Sorry. I'll see you guys later." Charity blushed as she let herself out the door.

"Back to you, young lady." Ulysses faced Ava.

"You make it sound like I'm in trouble."

"Not at all, but you have a decision to make." Ulysses folded his hands on the table. "Either you are willing to fight, to do whatever you have to do to win, or you need to find another role in the conflict. My initial offer is still open. It always will be; at least as long as we're still alive."

Ava felt conflicted. "When do I need to decide?"

"We have three days to plan an operation that should take weeks to work out. Let me know before supper." Ulysses closed the laptop. "I'd be more than content to pack up and go to Oklahoma. We can join up with the militia there and fight Markovich when he crosses into Alliance territory.

But you can't wear kid-gloves when you're fighting an insurgency battle. By definition, it's brutal. Insurgent tactics are the only way an inferior force can take a stand against a stronger enemy."

Ava looked at Foley hoping he would provide her with the words of wisdom she needed to make this decision. But she knew he could not. This answer had to come from inside. "I think I need some time alone. I'm going to get my pole and see if I can pull in some fish for dinner."

Ava watched the bobber float with the gentle current of the river, hoping nothing would take the bait. Ava spoke aloud, half to herself to hear her own thoughts, and half to her Creator, hoping for a divine solution to her internal quandary. "Foley and Dad have been tried and tested in the fires of war. They've seen unimaginable savagery committed by human beings against one another.

"They became battle-hardened by fighting people who don't talk like us, dress like us, or have anything in common with our culture. I suppose that shouldn't make any difference, but somehow, it seems harder to kill someone who eats at the same restaurants you eat at and watches the same TV shows as you."

She huffed. "I don't know. I didn't feel right bombing those collection points. I don't feel right about this. But I don't think I can live with myself if I sit back and let Markovich and his minions take away our freedoms unopposed. Communism always ends with religious persecution. This is about so much more than politics or economics; it's about being free to worship God. But who will I become if I have to act like a murderous brute or a homicidal fiend in order to preserve that freedom?"

Ava looked up at the clouds above, wanting to see a sign that God was listening, that He had an answer. She let her gaze drop back down at the bobber, which was perilously close to getting caught in the grass on the bank of the river.

She considered letting it be, but at the last minute, she stood up from the bench and began fervently reeling it in and away from the inevitable weedy trap of complacency. "I guess inaction can be even more detrimental to my humanity than what I might consider *ruthless action*." The bobber skipped away from the hazard of being trapped by the weeds. "And I suppose I have my answer."

# CHAPTER 21

The horse is prepared against the day of battle: but safety is of the Lord.

Proverbs 21:31

Friday morning, Ava looked in the bathroom mirror and cut the first strand of hair. "Oh, this is going to be harder than I thought. Besides, if I do it myself, it's going to look like I did it myself." She placed the scissors on the sink next to the black hair dye and went to look for Charity.

Not seeing her anywhere in the house, she crossed the yard to the garage. Ava opened the side door and climbed the stairs to the FROG.

Charity sat up on the bed by the window and brushed her hair with her fingers. James blushed. He'd obviously not been guarding the driveway with his full attention.

"What's up?" Charity scooted a few feet away from her husband.

Ava looked at the two of them. "Sorry, I should have knocked."

"We were just . . . talking." Charity smiled.

Ava lifted her eyebrows. "Sure. When you're finished . . . talking, I need some help with my hair."

"Why? What's wrong with your hair?" Charity asked.

Ava rolled her eyes. "It looks just like the hair of that terrorist chick that the news is blaming all those bombings on. I wouldn't want anyone to confuse me with her."

"Oh, totally." Charity stood up. "I can help you. We weren't talking about anything important."

"Thanks." Ava paused before going down the stairs to look at James. "This won't take long. You two can get right back to your . . . conversation."

He looked through the rifle scope toward the front gate, as if to avoid eye contact with Ava. "No trouble at all. Take your time."

Once in the bathroom, Charity asked, "So, what are we doing today?"

Ava chuckled, "What, are you a salon stylist now?"

Charity picked up the scissors from the sink. "I'm the closest thing to a stylist that you've got. Come on, let's do this outside so we don't have such a mess to clean up." She grabbed the box of hair dye. "Black? You know who you're going to look like, right?"

"If you're going to say Raquel, forget it. I'd have to go on a six-week crack binge to look like her." Ava followed Charity out to the backyard and sat on a stump.

"How short do you want it?"

"Chin length."

"Like Raquel's?"

"Stop saying that!"

Charity giggled and began clipping Ava's beautiful auburn hair.

Ava sat still. "Sorry I can't tell you what all of this is about."

"I don't even want to know." Charity held Ava's hair between her fingers and cut another section. "I saw Foley and your dad over by the range playing with a drone. They were duct taping something to it, trying to get it balanced or something. I don't have to use much imagination to guess what they're up to. I wish I could un-see that. But anyway, I'm glad I'm sitting this one out."

"Lord willing, we'll have many more opportunities." Ava watched the clumps of hair fall to the ground.

"Yeah, well, you just be safe. Come back to me." Charity made a series of clips. "Any idea when you're leaving?"

"This evening."

"When do you think you'll be back?"

"Monday or Tuesday. You might hear about us on the news before that. We may have to lay low for a couple days, so I can't give an exact date for our return. Dad thinks roadblocks could be up, people looking for us on the way home."

"Wow! I am glad to be staying home." Charity fluffed her hair. "How does that feel?"

"Short."

"That's what you asked for."

"I know. Let's do the color and get it over with."


Two hours later, Ava put on her hoodie and her thick black-framed Wayfarer reading glasses. The lenses had minimal magnification, which slightly affected her long-range vision, but they were only for her disguise and wouldn't be on long enough to matter. She pulled a black skull cap over her head, which pushed down her new jet-black bangs to her eyebrows. Ava put on her red armband and went to the garage to find Foley.

She quietly climbed the stairs and looked at him lying prone on the bed with his eye to the rifle scope.

He seemed to have heard someone coming up the stairs and turned to look behind. Foley's body jerked when he saw her and he sat up instantly swinging the rifle around.

Ava began laughing. "I guess if it fooled you I shouldn't have any trouble walking into the SJL demonstration."

Foley closed his eyes and exhaled deeply, putting his hand on his chest. "Don't ever do that! What if I had shot you?"

"You're not going to shoot me." She leaned in for a kiss.

He pulled her in close for a moment then pushed her back to get a better look.

"Do you like it?"

He bit his lip. "No, but it's for a good cause."

"The black will fade in a few weeks then I can recolor it."

"Back to the original?"

"That might take a little longer, but we can start working in that direction."

"And the length?"

"A few months. Wow, you really don't like it, *do you*?" She examined the sad expression on his face.

"You were, I mean you *are* my dream girl. I love you no matter what, but your hair was hot the way it was."

She fought a grin. "You should have told me before."

He hugged her.

She kissed him again. "And I love you, too."

His smile grew wider as they kissed.

She giggled and pulled back. "What?"

"You said it back this time."

"This time?"

"The last time I told you I loved you, you didn't say it back."

"You never told me you loved me before. Even this time it was veiled in a delayed, indirect compliment of sorts."

"What are you talking about?" He kept his arms around her waist. "I told you flat out that I was falling in love with you."

She made a tisking sound. "*I'm falling in love with you* is not the same as saying *I love you*."

"Oh, come on!" he protested.

"Shhhhhh." She put her finger on his lip and kissed him again.

Minutes later, he stood up. "I thought we'd agreed not to do this up here anymore."

"You're right. I better go before we get ourselves in trouble." Ava picked up her glasses and headed to the stairs. "See you at lunch?"

"Yeah, James is relieving me." He grabbed his rifle and sat back down on the bed. "I wish you didn't have to go."

"Me, too." She twirled the drawstring of her hood around her finger then forced herself to start down the stairs.

After lunch, Ava met with Ulysses and Foley in the trailer.

"I told Sam we're leaving and that I wasn't sure when we'd be back, but hopefully by the middle of next week." Ulysses made the final preparations to the explosive device Ava would be carrying into the Social Justice Legion demonstration.

Ava watched as he tucked it into the black backpack. "You're not putting any shrapnel on the charge like the ones we used at the collection points?"

"No." Ulysses zipped up the pack. "Right Now could be protesting nearby. If I add shrapnel, it could hit one of them. This device is more about noise than destruction.

"All the green spaces around the stadium have trees. When you get to the demonstration, drop your pack by a tree then blend in with the demonstrators. Chat, yell, clap, whatever they're doing. Then watch the time. One minute before the drone is set to go off, start walking away. Once you hear the explosion, give the demonstrators a few seconds to look at each other and wonder what's going on. Then detonate your device. That will be Foley's cue to open fire.

"Start running after you detonate, because that's what everyone else will be doing. I'll leave the parking lot of the mall as soon as my drone blows up. So, you should see me driving right by you. But if something happens to me, you'll have to get to Foley's location for your evac."

Ava held the pack to feel the weight of the explosive inside. "How will I know if you get cut off? You and Foley will be the only ones with earbuds in. My phone will just be set up for you guys to hear me."

Foley answered. "I'll know if something happens to Ulysses. If you don't see him when you get to the road, check your phone. If something is up, I'll send you a text that says *Plan B*. Then you'll know to head in my direction."

Ava looked at her father to see if he'd sign off on Foley's idea.

"That will work." Ulysses nodded. "When we leave from here, I'll be pulling the trailer which will be carrying all of the explosives. You two will follow behind in Foley's Ford. Ava, you drive. Foley, you'll ride shotgun. If you see I'm getting tailed, call me on the radio and let me know. We'll come up with a plan when we know what we're up against."

"Where are we going to leave the trailer when we initiate the attack?" Foley asked.

Ava answered, "Lake Livingston, north of

Houston, has campgrounds around it. I doubt they're very busy in mid-December, especially if that area has no electricity. It might be a good place to lay low for a few days. Plus, if the regime thinks we're the ones responsible for the attack, they'll probably focus their roadblock efforts between the attack site and Taylor, assuming that's where they think our base of operations is located."

Ulysses opened his laptop and typed on the keyboard. He waited for the information to come up. "Lake Livingston is over an hour away from the stadium." He stared at the screen. "But I don't see any better alternatives. We'll have to get out of the area fast before they lock down the roads out of Houston."

He spun the laptop around and pointed at a spot near the lake. "This is our destination. Jot down directions if you need them." He stood up to get a pen and a piece of paper.

Ava drew a crude map. "Got it."

Ulysses closed the laptop. "Say goodbye to your friends and load up your gear. We'll roll out in an hour."

"We're going to the lake now?" Ava asked.

"Yeah. We'll spend the day there tomorrow. That gives us a chance to see who else is around us. If it doesn't look good, we'll find another location to leave the trailer."

"What about Buck?" Ava asked.

"He comes with us. We'll need him to keep curious people away from the trailer while we're in Houston. And, we'll need him to let us know if anyone is slipping up on us after we return. Bring plenty of dog food and lots of treats. He's our number one watchman. I want him to be happy."

Ava smiled. "I can handle that."


Ava knocked before going upstairs to the FROG where Charity was keeping James company while he was on watch.

"Come on up," Charity called.

Ava climbed the stairs. "Hey, we're heading out. I'll see you when I see you."

James stood up, rifle in hand. "I want to pray for your team before you go."

"That's so nice. We'd be very grateful for that," Ava said.

"Hopefully no bad guys show up while I'm away from my post." James led the way downstairs.

Charity trailed behind him. She turned to look at Ava. "I'll get Sam and Betty. I know they'll want to say goodbye."

Ava and James walked to the trailer where Ulysses and Foley were stowing the last of their gear.

"I feel bad that I'm not coming along," James said to Foley.

"You'll be back in the game soon enough. But you need to wait for those wounds to finish healing." Foley inspected the stitches on James' face and neck. "And you'll be the head of security while we're gone. Without Buckley around, that will be a full-time job."

Ulysses walked up to James and nodded his agreement. "You're a fine soldier. You've served your country well in the last two operations. You have nothing to feel bad about. Like Foley said, heal up and you'll be ready to go on the next run." He watched as Charity came out of the house with the Hodges behind her. "Taking care of your wife and the base is an honorable task. We all feel better knowing you're here to look after things."

"Thank you." James shook his hand.

Betty handed two large plastic bags to Ava. "Y'all take these with you."

Surprised by the weight, Ava said, "Wow! What's in here?"

"Steaks and pork chops. I cooked them on the grill. You've also got some mayonnaise and bread to make sandwiches."

"Thanks, but we'll never eat all of this."

"Without electricity, everything in that freezer is going to go bad. Give some to Buckley. I'm sure he can eat half of it."

"We appreciate it, Betty," Ulysses said. "But if you keep the freezer door closed, we might be back before everything thaws out. As long as I have fuel, I can keep the batteries in the trailer charged off of the truck."

"Well, y'all need to eat anyways." Betty gave Ava a big hug.

Sam took one of the bags and helped Ava carry it into the trailer. "Betty and I are both proud that we've been able to support you and your team. I know it's not much, but it makes us feel good to know we're involved in trying to take back Texas."

Ava squatted down to make room in the small refrigerator of the tiny trailer kitchenette. "Your help has been absolutely instrumental in giving us the support we need. None of this would have been possible without your and Betty's assistance." She finished packing the food and stood back up. "Thank you so much, Sam. For everything."

He hugged her. "Betty and I never had kids, but if we had, I'd have wanted a girl just like you."

Ava squeezed him tightly. "Before Ulysses came along, you were the closest thing I knew to a father. I wish I'd told you that before."

"Better late than never." He patted her on the back, then let her go. "You take care of yourself."

She nodded and walked back out of the trailer to join the others. Sam followed.

James took Charity and Betty's hands. "Let's all gather around, form a circle, and ask God to protect our friends as they go do what they feel He is leading them to do."

Ava took Ulysses and Foley's hands. She bowed her head.

"Lord," said James. "We ask for your providence, courage, and protection for this team. A godless foe has risen up against this nation. It has been a long time coming, but now the day is here. It is time for your sons and daughters to draw a line in the sand and say *no further* to the enemy.

"We have suffered far too many encroachments against the law which you ordained through our Constitution, and far too many trespasses against your way and your Word. The time for negotiating with the enemy has passed. No more can we go along to get along. Though we have tried to be people of peace, violence has been forced upon us.

"Grant Ava, Ulysses, and Foley the strength they

need to succeed in their quest. In Jesus' name, I pray, amen."

Ava hugged Charity one last time. "I'll see you soon."

"You're like a sister to me, Ava."

"Same here." Ava pushed Charity's blond hair out of her eyes and gave her one last embrace.

"Godspeed," Charity said.

Ava opened the back door of Foley's truck for the dog. She clapped her hands. "Buck, come on, boy! Time to roll out."

Buckley came running, seeming to be elated at the thought of yet another ride in the truck.

Ave closed the door for Buckley and got in the driver's seat. "Goodbye!" She waved.

# CHAPTER 22

Be anxious for nothing, but in everything by prayer and supplication, with thanksgiving, let your requests be made known to God; and the peace of God, which surpasses all understanding, will guard your hearts and minds through Christ Jesus.

Philippians 4:6-7 NKJV

Sunday morning, Ava sat in a soft pile of pine needles with her back against the trunk of one of the towering pines which surrounded the lakeside campsite. Buckley's head nuzzled deeper into her lap, providing her access to an area of his neck that had not yet been adequately scratched. She gazed out at the gentle ripples on the lake driven by the soft cool breeze. "This would have made a perfect vacation. But it's kind of hard to relax knowing what this day is going to be like."

The trailer door opened behind her. Foley stepped out wearing blue Dickies pants and a blue work shirt with the name *Bill* embroidered over the pocket.

Ava looked him over and grinned. "It's a fine day on the lake, ain't it, Bill?"

He came to sit beside her and Buckley. He ran his fingers through her short black hair. "People who live in glass houses shouldn't throw stones. My disguise isn't nearly so comical as yours."

"Like you said, it's for a good cause." Ava stroked Buckley's fur. "How are you planning to get on the roof?"

"I'll find the meter box and shut off the water."

"How's that going to get you on the roof?"

"I'll tell the front desk that we're doing emergency plumbing in the building next door and we accidentally tripped a pipe relay. I'll tell them that I need to reset it so we can turn the water back on."

"Tripped a pipe relay? Look, I know nothing about plumbing, but even *I* know there's no such thing as a pipe relay. And even if there were, you wouldn't access it from the roof."

"It's a computerized gauge that regulates water usage in order to conserve water. All older buildings were retrofitted with them last year. The roof is the only place they could be installed."

"You're making all of this up, aren't you?"

"You're fairly deft at critical thinking, but I

made you doubt, didn't I?" Foley winked at her. "Imagine a person educated by the common core public school system, who's working Sunday morning at the front desk of a hotel." Foley ticked off the additional factors of the scenario by raising one finger at a time. "One: you know the general manager isn't there on Sunday morning. Two: the maintenance man is on call for emergencies only. And three: the phone is ringing off the hook with guests wanting to know why their shower isn't working and telling you how bad they need to flush the toilet.

"Then I show up; a knight in slightly-greasy armor who's offering to make all your problems go away. It doesn't matter if the person knows there's no such thing as a pipe relay or not. The clerk will *want* to believe me. And the roof-access key card will be shoved into my hands with pleading eyes, begging me to just get it fixed fast."

Ava shook her head. "Did my dad cook up that one?"

"Concocted it myself."

"But he signed off on the ploy?" She lowered her chin and pressed her lips together.

"Yep. Why? You don't think it will work?"

"It probably will, but it takes real bravado to even come up with something like that, much less actually try to pull it off."

Foley looked out at the lake. "Less so than being America's most wanted and walking into an Antifa demonstration with only a box of hair dye and a pair of oversized glasses to hide your identity."

"With a bomb," she added.

"With a bomb," he echoed. "Aren't you nervous?"

"I am now that you've helped clarify the audacious risk I'm assuming here."

"Sorry." He took her hand.

"You don't think they'll be searching backpacks?"

Foley shook his head. "They can't search every car and person in a five-block radius. They'll be strict about what people bring into the stadium, but they don't have the manpower to control the outside.

"Woods will be whisked to the service entrance via a heavily-guarded convoy. He'll never be exposed to the outside of the stadium. They won't be worried about you."

"I hope you're right."

Ulysses walked up from the direction of the campground office. He held two cups with lids, stacked one on top of the other. "I brought you both some hot chocolate from the canteen." He handed them the cups then retrieved a package out of his jacket pocket. "And some powdered sugar donuts."

"Right on time. Thanks." Ava took the donuts and tore into them. This particular situation certainly merited a sugar splurge.

"Didn't you get any for yourself?" Foley asked.

"I did. I had mine in the canteen. The attendant was watching the news on television. I wanted to see what was going on. Plus, I wanted to feel out the attendant. He lives here and he's the only one running the campground."

"What impression did he give you?" Ava sipped

her hot chocolate.

"Oh, he hates Markovich alright. I doubt he'll ever suspect we had anything to do with this afternoon's news, but if he does, it's unlikely he'd say anything."

"We'll be gone when the attacks happen, and we'll return roughly an hour and a half later. It wouldn't be too difficult to figure out." Foley snatched a donut from Ava when she wasn't looking.

"The attendant pays more attention to the television than who's coming and going. He's just passing time." Ulysses looked at his watch. "We'll roll out in fifteen minutes. Foley, you'll go first in your truck. I'll leave about a minute behind you, to draw less attention from the campsite attendant. We'll stagger our reentry to camp as well. Stop at that gas station up the road and top off your tank. I'll meet you there and do the same. Once we return this afternoon, I don't want to leave camp again until we head back to Sam's."

Ava finished her donuts and hot chocolate under the giant pine tree. Then, she brought Buckley inside the trailer, filling his food and water bowls. "You keep an eye on things around here, Buck. We'll be back soon." Ava hoped she was speaking the truth.

An hour and a half later, Ulysses drove his old truck up Kirby Drive. "Foley's on the roof. He'll be in position soon. I'll let you out on the other side of the pedestrian bridge. That looks like the place where all your comrades are congregating. I'll be in the strip mall parking lot in two minutes." Ulysses looked at his watch. "Set your timer on your phone. Flight time for my drone is less than a minute. You need to drop the pack and be walking away three minutes from now. Keep your finger on the trigger, blow your charge a few seconds after you hear the drone detonate.

"Are you ready?"

"Ready as I'll ever be. Godspeed." Ava pulled her skull cap lower on her head and her black bandana up over her mouth. She put her glasses on, stepped out of the vehicle, and slung the deadly backpack over her shoulder.

"I love you," Ulysses said.

"I love you, too, Dad." Ava swallowed hard and closed the door.

Ava marched toward the center of the Social Justice Legion's demonstration area. Hundreds of black-clad youths gathered around the green spaces between the stadium and Kirby Drive. Many of them lined the street carrying professionally-made picket signs. Some read, *Join the Revolution*, while others said, *This is What Social Justice Looks Like*, and still others displayed stenciled images of Lenin, Che, or the hammer and sickle.

As Ava approached the crowd, she held her fist in the air to mimic the actions of the other demonstrators. She joined in the chant which was just starting. "The right is wrong! The right is wrong! The right is wrong!"

A tall lanky guy walked up to her. He looked her over from head to toe as if to admire her figure. Most of the girls in the crowd seemed to be either obese or anorexic. The young man pulled his hammer-and-sickle bandana down to speak to her. "Hey, just getting here?"

"Yeah," she said dismissively.

"We've got more signs over by the fence if you want one."

Ava took out her phone to look at the timer. "Maybe when I get back. I'm going to have to find a bathroom soon."

"I haven't seen any port-a-pots. And you can't get in the stadium without a ticket. You'd probably have to go to that strip mall up the road."

Ava looked around. "Yeah, I guess I'll do that. I'm waiting for my girlfriend."

"Oh." The guy's eyes sank, as if he'd just dropped his lucky quarter down a sewer drain.

Ava instantly understood why. "She's not *my girlfriend.* She's my friend and she's a girl, so, you know."

His eyes resuscitated. "Oh, right; yeah."

Ava said, "Her name is Jenny. She's really cute. You'll like her."

"Cool." He nodded nervously. "I'm Delaney."

"Nice to meet you. I'm Mackenzie."

He shook her hand. "I heard the leader is going to be asking for recruits to join the army. Normally, that wouldn't be my thing, but with everything that's going on, I'm thinking of signing up. What about you?"

Ava nodded pensively. "I don't guess it's fair to want a revolution and not be willing to get my hands dirty. Maybe we'll end up serving together."

Delaney smiled with excitement. "Yeah, that

would be cool."

Ava looked at her phone again. She had less than a minute to begin walking away.

"Did Jenny text you?" Delaney inquired.

"No. But I don't think I'm going to be able to wait much longer." Ava pulled the pack off her back and retrieved two water bottles from inside. "Do you want a water?"

"Sure." Delaney took it from her.

Ava opened her water and took a sip. "Would you mind keeping an eye on my pack while I'm gone? It's full of water and I don't want to cart it back and forth to the restroom."

"Sure. Do you want me to wear it?" he offered.

"No," she said a little too loudly. "No, don't bother yourself. I'll just leave it by the tree."

He nodded. "It'll be fine. I don't think anyone would bother it, but I'll watch out for it just in case."

Ava checked her timer again. "Jenny sent me a text. She's on her way. She's about my height, blonde hair. If you see someone who fits that description looking around, tell her I'll be right back."

Delaney smiled. "You got it."

"See ya." Ava gave him a flirty smile and walked away.

She sprinted across the street and looked up to see the drone passing overhead. Ava took a deep breath and braced herself for the explosion about to come.

BOOOM! The blast echoed through the air.

Ava turned to look at the protestors. Since the

explosion was so far up, they were startled but not running and screaming. All of them were quietly murmuring amongst themselves. The ones with demonstration signs let them fall to the ground as they looked at one another with dismay.

Delaney yelled across the street. "Are you alright?"

Ava waved him off and nodded. "I'm fine."

"Maybe I should come with you," he yelled, then turned to retrieve the backpack.

Ava's heart stopped. "Oh no!" She put her finger on the trigger. She did not have the heart to detonate the bomb and blow up someone who was trying to help her, even if he was an enemy soldier in waiting. "Please, no!" She watched as he pulled the straps of the pack over his shoulders.

Ava knew the mission could not fail. This was bigger than her, bigger than Delaney. In all likelihood, he'd have been killed by the blast anyway. Or perhaps he'd only have been severely maimed. At least this way, it would be quick and certain.

But if she was going to do it, she had to push the button before he turned around. She knew it would be impossible to look him in the eyes while she blew him to smithereens.

Delaney hoisted the weight of the pack evenly on his shoulders and began to turn around to face her.

Ava turned away, shielding her face from the death and destruction she would soon unleash. A sense of sickness reverberated from her hand which was holding the detonator. The icky sensation traveled up her arm and down into the pit of her stomach. She quivered at the thought of what she was about to do.

Click.

KABOOOOM!!!

She let the detonator rest inside her pocket and turned to face the carnage she'd just created. People were screaming, bloodied, and running in every direction. Several of the people lay motionless on the lawn. Three bodies had been tossed into the street by the blast. One girl stood screaming, bathed in red and missing her arm. Delaney was nowhere to be found.

Ava was horrified by what she'd done. So much so, that she felt unembodied like she didn't know the person in whom her mind now resided. She did not run. She did not turn. She forced herself to look on as a form of self-imposed punishment. Frozen in place, unable to move she witnessed the butchery and gore she'd unleashed.

Gunfire rang out from the distance. While she stood paralyzed by her own barbarity, Foley was unchaining yet another wave of slaughter. *Who have I become? Who are these people I'm with? What have I done?*

Ulysses' pickup stopped in the street, right between Ava and the massacre, blocking her view.

"Get in!" Ulysses reached over and pushed the passenger's side door open.

Ava did not move, did not blink.

Ulysses jumped out, ran to the other side and pushed her into the vehicle. He closed her door and rushed back to the driver's seat. He shoved the shifter into gear and sped away.

Ulysses jerked the earphones out of his phone and put it on speaker. "Foley, we're coming to you! What's your status?"

"On my way down right now."

"Roger that." Ulysses raced south on Kirby while three police cars with lights flashing drove the other direction.

Seconds later, Ulysses said, "Foley, I'm passing beneath the underpass. I need to know that you are at least in your vehicle and out of the parking lot before I get on the interstate. If you get in a pinch, I'd have a hard time helping you."

"Taking the stairs, sir. I've got one flight remaining. Truck's right outside." Foley sounded winded.

"Roger. I'll slow my pace." Ulysses turned left onto the I-610 frontage road.

Ava said nothing. Her mind was overloaded.

Ulysses drove past the first on-ramp and crossed Fannin Street.

"I'm on the road. Coming up on the underpass now," Foley said.

"Good! Stay back a few car lengths, but close enough for me to see you." Ulysses took the next on-ramp heading west onto I-610.

No one spoke for the next half hour. The escape route took them north onto I-69 and directly through downtown Houston. Tensions were high. Ulysses' knuckles turned white gripping the steering wheel.

Once they passed the airport, Ulysses let out a sigh and loosened his grasp. "We're a good twenty-five miles away from the stadium. Our odds of getting away are improving by the second. But I need you to be ready to engage if we get in trouble."

Ava stared blankly out the front windshield.

"This is what I was trying to explain to you. War changes you. It changes how you see things, what you think about yourself, and the way you feel about everyone else. People can tell you all about it, but until you've felt it for yourself, you don't really know what they're talking about.

"I never wanted this for you, Ava."

She listened quietly in her pain. Her lip quivered. Her chin wrinkled. The first tear to race down her cheek was soon followed by many more.

She remained silent and motionless except to wipe her face with her sleeve every few minutes.

A half an hour later, Ulysses checked his rearview, then exited the interstate. The rural roads which would take them back to camp were lined with trees and fences, cattle and fields. Farmhouses and an occasional building dotted the peaceful landscape.

Ava fixated on a small country church as they drove by. She broke her silence. "I'm a monster."

"You're not," Ulysses rebutted.

"I blew that kid up. He was only trying to help me."

"Ava, I don't know exactly what happened back there, but no one in that gathering had any legitimate intention of helping you. Especially if they'd known who you really were."

She sobbed louder, trying to speak between her wails. "Some guy, Delaney was his name, he offered to watch my pack." She wiped her tears with her sleeve and sniffed in a labored breath.

"When the drone detonated, he tried to pick up my pack and bring it to me." Her face contorted with sorrow and guilt. "And I blew him up."

Ulysses reached across the seat to put his hand on her knee. "You did what you had to do."

She shook her head and cried. Ava pulled her legs toward the door and away from her father's touch.

Ulysses put his hand back on the wheel. "Our tactics are unconventional. They're vicious in their appearance, but that kid isn't any more dead than if you'd shot him with a rifle. Actually, it was far less painful for him than dying from a gunshot wound.

"I understand it doesn't look that way to you. The explosion, it was shocking. That's part of the design. Our ultimate goal is to break the will of the enemy. It's the only way we win."

"Nobody is gonna win." Ava turned her head toward the side window. "And I'm a cold-blooded murderer."

Ulysses kept his face forward. "Let's unpack that. And we'll start with the cold-blooded part. How many cold-blooded killers do you suppose have a crisis of conscience like the one you're having right now?"

Ava said nothing.

"It's not a rhetorical question. Give it a stab. 50 percent? 30 percent? 10 percent? I'm waiting."

She shook her head. "I don't know."

"I do."

She didn't respond.

"Do you want to know the answer?"

"Whatever."

"Either you want to know or you don't. You're convicting yourself of heinous crimes against humanity over there in your seat. I'd think you'd want the data so you can formulate an informed verdict. After all, juries often decide cases based on what a reasonable person would do. If you're going to condemn my daughter, I'd at least like to make sure she gets a fair trial."

"A reasonable person wouldn't have done what I did."

"Ah! You're jumping to conclusions. We need to hear all of the evidence. No courtroom in the country would allow a trial to be so abbreviated."

She huffed. "Okay. What was the question?"

"What percentage of cold blooded killers experience a crisis of conscience after they've slain their victims?"

"I don't know. Tell me."

"Exactly zero. The very definition of cold blooded implies that a person feels no remorse for their actions. So, we can at least take that adjective off the table, right?"

"Fine." She crossed her arms and continued to watch the countryside pass by the window. "I'm an empathetic murderer."

"We're moving in the right direction. Are you familiar with stand your ground laws, castle doctrine, all of that?"

Ava glanced at her father. "Yeah. Lee, my adoptive mom's ex-husband, was a lawyer. I couldn't write out the legal definition of either one, but I understand the basic concept. But this isn't self-defense. I went to them!" She made a fist and turned away. "And killed them."

"Are you sure about that?"

"What do you mean?" She glared at him.

"Are you sure you went to them? You don't believe your country was invaded by communists? You don't think the law of the land was usurped by these very same people, when they beat people up to keep them from voting? In your mind, that doesn't qualify as a violent invasion, or at the very least a military coup to overthrow the legitimate American government?"

She was silent for a long while. Ava pondered what her father was saying. It was the very same argument she'd used on Sam, Betty, Charity, James, Foley, even her father whom she'd only moments earlier labeled as a monster eviler than herself. Ava was confused. She wanted to be mad at herself, at her father for devising the plan, and at Foley for going along with it. "Even so, it's not my job to bring them to justice."

"That's the attitude that got us here in the first place. Think about all of the pastors in America who were concerned with new building projects, bigger HD screens, better coffee shops, everything except the things that really mattered. They didn't think it was their job to stand up against wickedness. They saw no responsibility to defend freedom; felt no obligation to spur their congregations on toward fighting back against the far left.

"Stop me if this sounds familiar. After all, I'm simply rephrasing your material. You're the one who told me it was the armchair conservatives that sat idly by while God was evicted from the classroom and replaced by atheism.

"The only thing necessary for evil to prevail is for good people to do nothing."

Ava shook her head with her arms crossed. "I was wrong. I shouldn't have said what I said. And you shouldn't have listened."

"You weren't wrong," he replied. "You simply didn't understand the cost of your conviction. But nothing worth having is ever cheap, free, or easy."

She remained silent.

Ulysses left her alone for several minutes, then broke the silence. "Jefferson said, 'The tree of liberty must be refreshed from time to time with the blood of patriots and tyrants.' That sounds like he thought it was our responsibility."

"One man's opinion. Not law."

"How about the second amendment. 'A well-regulated Militia, being necessary to the security of a free State, the right of the people to keep and bear Arms, shall not be infringed.' Guns and militia are necessary to keep the state free. It goes without saying that the violence which accompanies guns and militia are also integral. That is every citizen's responsibility. And it's not some guy's opinion, it's the law.

"I'll spare you the dissertation on how your backpack bomb, while more effective, has the same fundamental goal as your rifle. You already know that. And I won't dismiss the ferocity of such a weapon. Using a weapon with that much destructive power is not an easy thing to do. It's not an easy thing to see done. It will take you a while to process it.

"Once you get to the other side of what you're going through, you may decide it's time to cash out. That will be okay. You've done your part. You've done more than most. We can still go back to Oklahoma and support the Alliance States logistically. They'll need food. Armies run on bread, lead, and gold. No one fights on an empty stomach. At least not for long."

Ava remained hushed until they pulled into the drive of the campground. "I'm ready."

"For what?"

"To leave. I'm ready to leave Texas. I want to go to Oklahoma with you. I can't do what I did today. I can't ever do anything like that again."

Ulysses nodded as he reached over to pat her on the thigh. "Like I told your friends back at Sam's, they're all invited."

"Thank you." Ava looked in the side view mirror at Foley's truck pulling in behind them. "I'm going to walk Buck, then get cleaned up and go to bed."

"If you need to be alone, that's fine. I won't bother you, and I'll make sure Foley knows. But you need to eat. All that stomach acid you've got going will eat a hole in your gut."

"I'll make a sandwich to eat while I'm walking Buckley." Ava picked up her rifle and hurried to the trailer. She heard Foley shut the door of his truck, but she avoided eye contact with him. She'd been a captive audience for her father on the ride home, but Ava had nothing more to say to anyone. Neither did she want to listen to anybody else.

# CHAPTER 23

Thou wilt keep him in perfect peace, whose mind is stayed on thee: because he trusteth in thee. Trust ye in the Lord for ever: for in the Lord Jehovah is everlasting strength: For he bringeth down them that dwell on high; the lofty city, he layeth it low; he layeth it low, even to the ground; he bringeth it even to the dust.

Isaiah 26:3-5

Monday morning, Ava sat on the ground near the bank of Lake Livingston, looking out at the water. Buckley lay at her side quietly, as if he knew she was troubled. Ava appreciated the fact that he wasn't trying to console her with words of wisdom.

She heard the trailer door open. She could tell by the footsteps that it was Foley. Ava wished she had a do-not-disturb sign to hang around her neck.

"I brought you coffee."

She said nothing, did not look at him.

"I can leave it here."

She knew punishing him would not make her feel better. "That's okay. You can sit down if you want."

Foley sat on the other side of Buckley and passed the cup to Ava. "How did you sleep?"

"I didn't."

"I tossed and turned all night, also. I always do after I'm involved in any type of action."

"I kept seeing the bomb blow up in my mind. I kept hearing the screams; and that kid. I won't ever forget it."

"Probably not, but the memory will get less vivid with time. It will fade, and it won't be so haunting."

She took a sip from the cup. "Thanks for the coffee."

"That's what we do. We take care of each other. Take some time. Work through things, but don't check out on me, okay?"

"Yeah. I guess my dad told you I'm having a hard time."

"I heard the conversation over the phone. We were connected the whole way home, remember?"

"Oh, right. I was so freaked out, I didn't even think of that. I'm a real mess, huh?"

"You're having a normal reaction to a very abnormal situation. And when you get ready, I'll be here to talk. You can't bottle all this up. Pain shared is pain divided."

"What's that supposed to mean?"

"It means when you share the pain you feel inside, you shed a chunk of it off. Just talking about it reduces the weight you'll be packing around in the days and weeks to come. It's hard to open up, but it really does help. For a lot of the guys I was in Syria with, it was the difference between life and death. The guys who opened up, they made it. The ones who didn't . . ." Foley shook his head. "A lot of those guys aren't around. Or if they are, they aren't really functioning on a human level. And of course, you know my story."

Ava couldn't imagine that anyone else on the planet had ever felt the way she was feeling. "You heard what Ulysses said to me?"

Foley nodded. "Your dad."

"Yeah, whatever."

"It's not whatever. The tendency is to alienate and isolate. By calling him by his first name, you're pushing him away, even if you don't realize it."

"Okay, my dad."

"I'm not trying to beat you up. It's just that I've seen this movie; nearly a hundred times. If you can simply see what's happening, what the Devil is trying to push you into, you can be better equipped to mitigate it."

"Thanks, I guess." Ava ran her hand through her too short, too black hair. "But I don't feel like it's the Devil. I feel like God is angry with me, that I've committed the unpardonable sin."

"That's not God. Revelation 12 identifies Satan as the accuser of the brethren. What your dad said to you on the way home yesterday was all true."

"I know. But that's from man's standpoint. Jesus told us to turn the other cheek and love our enemies."

"You can love them, you can pray for their salvation, but when you have an enemy trying to eradicate everything we hold dear, that's not what Jesus was talking about when he said to turn the other cheek.

"Make no mistake, the Social Justice Legion flies a flag with the hammer and sickle, just like their predecessor, Antifa. If communism takes root in America, it will outlaw churches, Bibles, and Christianity entirely. If it doesn't this will be the first time in history that a communist revolution hasn't banned every mention of God. It is a militaristic, atheistic system that does not make compromises or allowances.

"Turning the other cheek is about disregarding an insult. No one ever died from being slapped on the cheek. Jesus did not intend for you to lie down and let people run all over you.

"Jesus said the greatest commandment was to love the Lord your God with all of your heart, mind, and soul. He said the second is like it; to love your neighbor as yourself. That's the golden rule. Do unto others as you'd have done unto you.

"In the light of the second greatest commandment, consider this. If you did not know Jesus, wouldn't you want someone to stand up to Markovich and protect your right to at least hear about Him, so you could make your own decision as to whether you wanted to follow Christ or not?"

"Yeah, I suppose."

"Then you can't expect someone else to do it for you if you wouldn't do it for them. The God of the Old Testament not only consented to battles, He commanded the Israelites many times to completely wipe out their enemies. He's the same yesterday, today, and forever.

"Yes, God calls us to be merciful, but he also calls us to take a stand against evil. Like your dad said, it's the church's dereliction of that duty which has put us in the predicament we're in now. Twenty years ago, the Church could have come together to fight back in the political arena and spared us this battle. But now, it's too late; blood will be spilled.

"You've done your part. I believe God is very proud of your bravery. I don't think He is mad at you at all. Proverbs 31 tells us to take a stand for those who can't speak for themselves, to defend the poor and needy. That's what you did yesterday. While scores of men are hiding under their beds like cowards, you took a stand. Nothing is more righteous than that."

Ava listened and was quiet. She sipped her coffee and stared at the water. "Maybe you're right. But I'm done. I'm going to Oklahoma with my dad."

Foley nodded. "You've done your share of the heavy lifting."

She was silent for another long while. Then she said, "You could come with us."

Foley looked out at the slight waves. "I will. For a while, at least. I'm not sure I'll stick around the farm very long. I'll probably hook up with one of the militias."

Ava did not want him to go into battle anymore. She loved him and didn't want to worry every day, wondering if he was dead or alive. "To secure the border or to attack Markovich's forces?"

"I don't know. I wouldn't be in charge. But I have a certain skill set and it wouldn't be right if I didn't put it to use. I risked my life fighting in someone else's civil war. If I sit back when it is my own country, I think that would be a sin."

She swigged the end of her coffee. "You've been involved in all our missions. You said I've done enough. You've done everything I've done. Why can't it be enough for you?"

"It just isn't."

"I think it is. You said we take care of each other. You can't take care of me if you're not around." Ava's attention shifted from her self-loathing to worrying about Foley.

Ulysses came out of the trailer. "Did you tell her?"

Foley put his hands up. "We got to talking about other stuff, and I completely forgot."

"Tell me what?" She turned to her father.

"Woods is dead. They're blaming it on us." Ulysses stood by the pine tree.

"What? Woods was nowhere around any of us!"

Foley shrugged. "They said he was hit by a bullet."

"Is it possible?" she asked.

"Not even remotely. I was targeting the center of that Antifa gathering on the lawn opposite from where you were. It's a false flag. One that suits

Markovich very well. He probably had Secret Service kill Woods; for the good of the country."

Ava considered the implications. "So Markovich is president? He gets the keys a month early."

"Yep." Ulysses nodded. "And Woods becomes a martyr."

Ava shook her head. "What's sick about the whole thing is that even if Woods had known Markovich was going to have him killed, he'd still have stayed on and sacrificed himself."

Ulysses said, "But the bad news is that they're really after our scalps now. We'll have to lay low, stay off the roads a little longer than originally planned. We'll see how the manhunt goes. Maybe we can head home Wednesday. The news cycle is pretty short these days. A lot can happen between now and Wednesday."

Her father turned to go back to the trailer. "In the meantime, I'm going to get a big stack of pancakes going. Even if you don't feel like it, you need to eat, Ava."

She forced a smile. "Thanks, Dad. I'll eat when they're ready."

# CHAPTER 24

Rejoice with them that do rejoice, and weep with them that weep.

Romans 12:15

Ava stretched her arms, waking from a long nap Wednesday. "Where are we?"

"San Marcos. Almost home." Foley cut the ignition. "We're going to gas up. Keep your eyes open. You're currently America's most wanted."

She yawned. "How long was I out?"

"Three hours, at least. You needed it." Foley stepped out of the truck and closed the door.

Ava surveyed the gas station. She saw her father three pumps down, fueling up his old truck, which was pulling the travel trailer. Their eyes met briefly, but Ulysses quickly turned away. Ava understood that if anyone were to spot her, Ulysses' element of surprise would be her only hope of escape. She watched Buckley in the back seat. He spun around to get comfortable for the remainder of their journey.

Minutes later, Foley stepped back inside. "All set."

"We really took the long way around." Ava took a sip of water from her sports bottle.

"Ulysses wanted to make sure we skirted Houston and Austin. Taylor, too, since that's probably where they're looking for you the hardest."

Ava slumped back down in the seat so to be harder to spot. "I don't think I've slept three hours straight since the attack."

"It will get better." Foley started the engine but waited for Ulysses to pull out of the filling station before putting the truck in gear. "The nightmares may not ever go away, but they'll get less frequent."

"I really wish you'd stay at Dad's place, once we get to Oklahoma. I don't think I'll sleep when you're gone."

Foley tightened his jaw. "Hopefully, I'll be able to join up with a crew nearby. If I'm on the border, that's not far at all."

Ava adjusted the ball cap on her head. "Dad's place is in the north-east corner of Oklahoma. It's at least 250 miles from the Texas border."

"That's not so far. I can be there in a few hours."

"Next week is Christmas."

"It sure doesn't feel like Christmas."

"Promise that you'll at least wait until after New

Year's to join a militia. You've done a lot. You've earned a break for the holidays." She reached across the seat and put her hand on his knee. "Please. For me."

"I can do that. I'll hang around until New Year's."

Ava hated the thought of being separated from Foley. But in the same way he'd respected her decision to get in and out of the war, she had to respect his. She switched the radio on. "Did I miss anything while I was out?"

"Insurgency attacks against Markovich's regime are happening all over the country. Kentucky, Tennessee, the Carolinas. Fort Rucker in Alabama has sided with the Alliance States. The base's leadership refuses to recognize Markovich as a legitimate commander in chief."

"How is that going to play out?" Ava asked.

Foley shook his head. "Who knows? Since Alabama hasn't officially sided with the Alliance, I'm guessing it will get messy."

"Still no word on Florida or Georgia joining up?"

"I suspect all the southern states are waiting for the others to make the call. No one wants to be the first to commit. All the Alliance states have at least one border shared with another Alliance state. That's one border they don't have to worry about getting attacked, and it's a way for them to get assistance if they're overwhelmed by an attack."

"Busy news day," Ava said.

"That's not all. Markovich had a big production in Washington for Woods' funeral. He turned it into the big enlistment rally that we upset in Houston. The only difference is this one was aired all over the country.

"He pledged to bring the perpetrators of the attack on the stadium to justice and to put an end to Blackwell's rebellion. You know how the media spins it. According to them, the Alliance-States movement is just some fantasy ginned up by a few kooks in the Pacific Northwest."

"Did the national media mention me specifically as being responsible for the bombing or Woods' death?"

"No. You're just wanted for questioning. If they name you as the attacker, then they'll look stupid if they don't catch you. Besides, they can't risk you popping up on the web, claiming responsibility for the attack but telling everyone that you had nothing to do with Woods' assassination. If the regime gives you street cred by labeling you as the mastermind, you'll become an icon; a living representation of the resistance."

"Well, I'm no icon."

"Maybe not. But you are brave. And you are a hero . . . or heroine, rather."

"I sure don't feel like it." She sat with her arms crossed.

"That's part of the reason that you are."

Ava stayed low in her seat for the rest of the trip back to Sam Hodge's farm. She watched the treetops pass by.

Once they made the last turn onto the county road, she asked, "Do you think Sam and Betty will come to Oklahoma?"

"They should, but I kinda doubt it." Foley glanced over at her. "What about James and Charity? Do you think they'll come?"

"Definitely. I know Charity will want to get out of here. I think James may be finished fighting, too."

"I don't know. James may surprise you. I think he might be a little gun shy from taking a shotgun blast to the face and neck, but I bet he'll get back in the saddle."

"If he does, it needs to be of his own accord. He doesn't need any goading from you," she said firmly. "I'd hate for Charity to go through the same worry I'm going to have to deal with."

Ava let out a deep sigh of relief as Foley turned into Sam Hodge's long driveway. They followed Ulysses up the gravel road to the house.

Ava saw her father exit the vehicle in front of them with his rifle in one hand and the other hand up in the air. Instantly, she knew something wasn't right. "The front door is wide open."

Foley grabbed his rifle. "Stay here."

Ava retrieved her rifle also. "I'm not getting separated from you and Dad, are you crazy?"

Foley spoke low. "Then at least make sure Buckley stays in the truck."

Ava closed the door gently and came around to the front of the pickup. She kept close to Foley as he hustled toward the front door where Ulysses waited to enter.

Her father nodded to Foley, then the two of them rushed into the house. Ulysses covered the stairwell leading up.

Foley penetrated into the living area and scanned the kitchen. "Two dead."

Ava looked through her reflex sight as she entered the kitchen. Sam and Betty Hodge were on the floor in a pool of dried blood. Flies buzzed around their corpses, signaling that they'd been killed days earlier.

Ava swallowed hard and trailed Foley while he cleared the remaining rooms downstairs.

After Foley searched the downstairs bathroom, he called, "All clear."

Ulysses said, "Stack up by the stairs."

Foley and Ava lined up behind Ulysses, who led the team up the stairs. One by one, they cleared each room, with Ava's bedroom being last.

"Clear." Ulysses lowered his rifle.

Ava walked into her room, which had been ransacked. On the wall, written in what looked to be blood, a message was inscribed. It said *you were warned.*

"Chip and Raquel," she said.

"How did they figure out you were staying here?" Foley asked.

Ava thought back to the shootout at the warehouse. "When Raquel was lying on the floor after the firefight. I suggested to Dad that we bring her to Sam to get her fixed up. She must have figured out this is where I was staying. It's my fault. I got them killed."

Ulysses held his rifle low and put his free hand around Ava. "Even if that's what happened, it's not your fault. Chip and that little witch killed Sam and Betty. But we'll talk about this later. We have to clear the garage, the barn, and the rest of the property. SJL could still have people here. I need you to keep it together and be brave for me right now. Can you do that?" He looked into her eyes, which were tearing up.

She swallowed hard again and nodded. "Yes." Ava pulled the butt of her rifle tightly against her shoulder.

Ulysses wiped her eyes with his thumb. "Okay. Let's go. Foley behind me. Ava behind Foley."

The team worked their way back down the steps, out the front door and moved quickly toward the garage. Ulysses opened the side door and led the way up the stairs to the FROG. Foley and Ava followed close.

"Clear." Ulysses lowered his rifle then went to the window and looked out.

Ava stood beside him. "No sign of Charity or James. Do you think they took them?"

"I don't know. We still have a lot of farm to cover." Ulysses finished surveying the property from the window and led the team back down the stairs.

All three of them kept their rifles up as they exited the side door of the garage. Ulysses started toward the garden. He put his hand up for them to stop.

Foley went to one knee. Ava followed suit.

Ulysses proceeded cautiously, pausing at what appeared to be another body lying face down in the grass. After inspecting his find, Ulysses waved them over.

Ava soon recognized the body to be James'.

Flies swarmed around his corpse, just as they had Sam and Betty's.

Ava's heart sank. Whether she found Charity dead, or if she'd been taken by Chip and Raquel's team, neither scenario offered a palatable outcome. Ava's fear melted away into sorrow and anger. "I can't believe Raquel did this. Sam tolerated her coming in late, showing up hungover; and that's what he got in return. I can't believe I let her live. I should have put a bullet in her skull at the warehouse. I should have put her out of her misery and mine."

Ava turned to her father. "And Chip. We should have taken him out before we left to Houston."

Ulysses looked around the farm. "We didn't have time. We can't go back and change the past. So, there's no use in debating how we could have done things differently. I spent thirty years learning that lesson, but believe me; it's true. Let it go and move on."

Ava looked at James' motionless body, face down in the grass. "I can't let it go. We have to get Chip. And we have to kill Raquel."

Ulysses glanced at her tight-lipped, then continued to watch the landscape surrounding them. He did not respond.

Foley kept his rifle at a low-ready position and watched the opposite direction. "She's right. This guy is never going to let this go. We have to take him out, or he'll follow us to Oklahoma."

Ulysses stared blankly for over a minute. Finally, he said, "We need to get Chip. But it can't be about revenge." He turned to Ava. "If you can't put that aside, you'll have to sit out. Foley and I will bring him in."

"It's not about revenge," Ava lied. "It's like Foley said, we have to take him out before he takes us out. And we have to get Raquel, also."

"First, we have to clear the property. Stay sharp." Ulysses raised his rifle and continued walking toward the animal pens.

When they approached the hog pen, Ava saw that the wild pigs were gone. The door had been left open. She heard the chickens clucking. They were out of the cage, but most of them appeared to still be in the vicinity.

Foley branched off from the group toward the rabbit hutches. "They let the bunnies go, too."

Ulysses checked inside the barn. "Clear." He lowered his weapon. "They may be back, but no one is around now."

Ava kept walking. She continued to the river's edge and walked the serene bank where she'd fished with Charity only days earlier. A glint of something in the bushes caught her eye. "Pink." She hurried over to the item. A sneaker was lodged in the mud. Ava pulled it out. "This is Charity's shoe, I'd recognize those pink laces anywhere." Ava gazed up the river in the direction the shoe was pointed. A breath of hope filled her lungs. She sprinted back to her father with the shoe.

"I think Charity may have gotten away." She held the muddy sneaker for him to see.

Ulysses looked toward the river.

Ava pointed south. "It looks like she followed the river. I think she might have gone down to

Riemer's Swimming Hole. The park has a restroom and a pavilion. It would be the only shelter she knew about. Since we kept the trailer there for the bombing raid on the collection points, she might think we'll go back there."

Ulysses nodded. "Foley, take Ava down to the park and check it out. I'm going to try to get these chickens back in the cage. I'd like to take them with us when we leave. I'm also going to get started on some graves. Once that's all finished, we'll dig up those AK-47s and get out of here. I don't want to be here when Chip comes back with his SJL squad. Keep your radio on."

"Yes, sir. We won't be gone long." Foley led the way back to his truck.

Ava opened the back door of the vehicle to let the dog out. "Stay with Dad, Buck." She closed the back door and took her seat up front.

Foley turned the truck around and headed back out the drive. The most direct route to the riverside park took them down a dirt road. A cloud of dust kicked up in the wake of the truck as Foley drove hard toward Riemer's Swimming Hole.

They arrived a few minutes later. Ava jumped out of the truck with her rifle ready for trouble. "Charity?"

Foley exited the vehicle in a much more cautious manner. He carefully scanned the area with his AR-15 at low ready.

The door to the small public restroom building creaked open. Ava tightened the stock of her rifle against her shoulder. "Charity?"

The girl peeked out the door. "Ava?"

"Are you okay?" Ava had to be sure this wasn't a trap and that no one else was behind the door before embracing her frightened friend. "Are you alone?"

Charity emerged from the facility. Her face contorted with sorrow as she began to weep.

Ava let the rifle hang by its sling and took hold of Charity. "It's okay." She nodded for Foley to double check the restroom, to be sure they were indeed alone.

Foley seemed not to need the cue as he was already walking toward the door.

"It was awful, Ava!" Charity spoke between sobs. "I was feeding the animals. I didn't take my rifle. I couldn't do anything. It's all my fault. James, Sam, Betty, they're all dead because of me."

"No. You didn't kill them. Chip and Raquel killed them." Ava held her tightly.

Foley came out of the restroom. "All clear."

Charity wailed for a long while. "They came in armored vehicles; five of them. They didn't stand a chance."

"Did you see Raquel?"

"Yeah, she was in the last vehicle with a really tall guy."

"That sounds like Chip."

"They didn't get out of the armored vehicle until the soldiers had already killed James. I hid in the bushes by the river. When Raquel and the guy got out I heard him order the soldiers to search the property. I didn't know where else to go, so I came here."

"What day was this?"

"Monday afternoon."

Ava pulled back enough to get a good look at Charity. "Did you have food and water?"

"No. The power is out, so there's no water in the restroom, but it did provide me with shelter. Yesterday, I gave in and drank water from the river."

"We've got water in the truck. Come on. Let's get you back. You can take a shower in Dad's trailer. I'll have something ready for you to eat by the time you're cleaned up."

Late Wednesday evening, Foley closed the Bible he'd been reading aloud from in the fading light. Charity placed a bouquet of wild flowers near the simple wooden cross, which marked James' grave. The long green stems with fluffy purple rods at the top were the only thing that distinguished James' final resting place from that of Sam and Betty's.

Ava cried for her friend who'd held the exact same flowers for her wedding only weeks earlier. Like bookends, the flowers marked the beginning and end of Charity's brief time of being one with her husband; one bouquet heralding such great joy, the other unspeakable sorrow.

Ulysses stood next to Foley. Both were filthy from having dug the graves and excavated the cached weapons behind the barn. Ulysses said, "Daylight is fading fast. We need to be gone before dark."

"You two don't want to get cleaned up first?" Ava asked.

"We don't have time. We need to leave. We're

very vulnerable being here at all. Darkness will make this place that much more dangerous."

Foley tucked the Bible under his arm. "Buchanan Lake is less than an hour away. It has a campground. Probably no electricity, but it's a place to park."

"Then that's where we'll go." Ulysses kicked the dirt off the shovel he still held in his hand. "Let's load up."

"Come on." Ava felt cruel pulling Charity away from James' gravesite so abruptly, but it had to be done.

Ulysses had put the chickens in the vacated rabbit hutches. The temporary cages were loaded into the back of Foley's truck along with a few scavenged items from the Hodges' farmhouse.

All the food and most of the other consumable provisions stored at the house had been taken by the SJL soldiers who'd come with Chip and Raquel. Ava drove Sam Hodge's GMC Sierra. Charity rode with her. Ava's team left very little behind except for the roof which had provided their shelter, the soil which they'd worked for food, and the terrible memories of the loss they'd just suffered.

# CHAPTER 25

But when they persecute you in this city, flee ye into another.

Matthew 10:23a

Thursday morning, Ava exited the travel trailer to walk Buckley. Like the campground at Lake Livingston, Black Rock Park on Buchanan Lake was empty except for Ava and her team. Unlike the Livingston Campground, Black Rock was officially closed, which meant the team could get unwanted attention if they were spotted. Ulysses chose the camping space farthest from the road.

Ava restrained Buckley's leash to keep him from wandering after his morning business had been settled. "Come on, Buck. Sorry, no exploring today." She led him back to the campsite.

Ulysses and Foley sat at the picnic table provided by the campground. "How's Charity?" Foley asked.

"Not good. She doesn't want to get out of bed."

"It's best that we leave her be." Ulysses folded his hands. "I doubt she got much rest during the two days she was hiding out in the public restroom. But let's make sure she stays hydrated. We won't know for sure whether she picked up anything from drinking river water for another day or so. If she does get sick, it will be easier for her to deal with if she's fully hydrated. Plus, keeping the water going will help flush out any potential toxins."

"I started her on a course of prophylactic antibiotics." Ava held the leash firmly and took a seat at the table.

"That will help if she was exposed to bacterial contaminants, but we have to think about viral pathogens, also. River water is a little different than a crystal-clear mountain stream. She could have chemical pollutants as well. The only thing you can do to mitigate that at this point is keep drinking clean water," Ulysses said.

Ava asked, "So, what are we going to do about Chip? Are we going to get him before we leave Texas?"

Foley looked at Ulysses before turning his attention to Ava. "We were discussing that before you walked up."

"Don't let me stop you. Please, continue." She gestured with her hand.

"Markovich has a full-scale manhunt going for you." Ulysses straightened his back. "I'm thinking it might be best if we took you and Charity across the border first. Foley and I can come back to collect the target."

"Without me?"

"The regime is making wallpaper with your mug shot, Ava. It's not safe for you anymore." Foley shook his head. "We need to get you into friendly territory."

"I've never been arrested, it's not a mug shot. It's my driver's license photo. But still, you're blowing it out of proportion."

"I disagree with you, Ava." Ulysses gave her a stern look. "We'll have to go into Austin to capture Chip. The majority of the population there would give you up in a second. They're mostly loyal to the regime."

"We'll go in at night."

"Yesterday morning, you were finished fighting. Why can't you let this go; sit this one out?" Foley quizzed.

"Because he killed my friends."

Ulysses shook his head. "I told you, this can't be about revenge."

"It's not revenge. It's justice. Besides, two people can't pull this off. His apartment will have a twenty-four-hour guard posted outside. He'll probably have SJL soldiers inside the building, also. You need me."

"We only have one silencer. I need to go back to Oklahoma to get more suppressed weapons anyway." Ulysses stood up to pace, as he often did when he was developing a plan.

Ava turned around to watch him walk about.

"That's a nine-hour drive each way. More if you plan on taking the backroads. Plus, you have to get across the border twice; no, three times. You'd save two days of driving and reduce the risk of getting caught at the border if you'd just snatch him up first, then take him with us. I think traveling back and forth is more likely to get you caught than the noise of gunfire. If the guards don't see us coming, one suppressed rifle will be enough."

Ulysses turned to Foley. "You look like you have something to say."

He raised his shoulders. "She has a point. It's a long trip, most of it through enemy territory. Making the run once is better than three times."

Ulysses grunted. "I need to mull this over. Why don't you two scratch up some breakfast? I may not think better on a full stomach, but at least I won't be so irritable. And make sure Charity eats. I'm going to take Buck with me for a walk along the lake. Come on, boy."

Ava watched Buckley quickly abandon her for Ulysses. "So much for my *faithful companion*. I thought Buck was different."

Breakfast consisted of eggs, oatmeal, and bread. Ulysses said nothing during the meager meal. Figuring that he was still contemplating what to do, Ava didn't prod him. Despite Ava's pleas, Charity did not get up to eat with the others. She remained in bed but did agree to drink some water and eat a bowl of oatmeal.

After breakfast, Ava and Foley walked hand-in-hand by the lake.

"Something is on your mind." Ava wrapped her free arm around Foley's.

"Wow. You're pretty observant. As boring as it's been around here, you'd almost have to be psychic to pick up on that one." A subdued grin broke out across his face.

"Shut up." She slapped his arm playfully. "I know you, Foley. You take all of this fighting and blowing stuff up like water off a duck's back. It's something else. Talk to me. You can't expect me to share my deepest darkest fears if you won't."

His face became more somber. "Now's not the right time to talk about it, but after yesterday, I'm afraid of it going unsaid."

"What are you talking about?"

He bent over to pick up a stone. He spun the smooth rock between his fingers. "Coming home to Sam, Betty, and James being dead; it made me realize how temporary life is; at least life on this planet."

"Go on." She waited for him to finish his thought.

"If something happens—to me . . . or you; I want you to know how I feel." Foley sent the stone skipping across the lake.

She hugged him. "I know, you love me. And I love you."

He pulled back from her embrace. "It's more than that. I want to spend the rest of my life with you. Whether it's two days or eighty years, win or lose, live or die, whatever time I have left on earth, I want to spend it with you."

Her heart fluttered, causing her to gasp. She

watched his hand go into his jacket pocket and come back out. Her pulse quickened. She felt faint.

Foley produced a ring made of wire that had been woven together in a beautiful pattern. "You deserve so much more than this homemade ring. If you say yes, and I'm around long enough, I'll get you the most beautiful diamond you've ever seen. Will you marry me?"

Ava covered her mouth and nodded. Her eyes welled up with tears. Ava knew all about engagement rings. The one Lee had given her adoptive mother held an absolutely stunning 1.5 carat diamond, but in the end, the commitment behind it didn't mean squat. In her mind, it was the promise represented by the ring which merited true value . . . or lack thereof.

She held out her hand, letting Foley slip the emblem of his affection on her finger. Only time would tell, but Ava actually believed that Foley would keep his pledge to her. She trusted him to hold to his vow, forsaking all others and 'til death do us part.

Later that evening, Ava sat at the picnic table with her father.

"Did he pop the question yet?" Ulysses inquired.

"What?"

"You've been very evasive with your left hand. I'm guessing you're trying to avoid the subject."

"How did you know?"

"Do you think that boy would ask you to marry him without coming to me first?"

Ava really hadn't considered that aspect. She'd

lived so many years without a real father that the idea of one being involved in this very monumental occasion had totally slipped her mind. "So, you approve?"

Ulysses ran his fingers through Buckley's fur on his head. "You're cut from the same cloth. You'll be good for each other—if we make it through all of this."

She considered his words. "Did you decide what we're going to do about Chip?"

"We'll pick him up tomorrow night." Ulysses answer was direct and quick.

Ava needed more details. "So, I'm on the team?"

Ulysses sucked his teeth, making a ticking sound, as if he was entirely uneasy about bringing Ava along. "You're on the team."

She kept her excitement contained. "We'll leave from here?"

"We will, but we won't come back here. I need you to speak with Charity. I'm going to hook the trailer up to the Sierra. We'll load up the chickens and all the supplies we can. We'll send her north; up past Wichita Falls. Little town called Byers; they're mostly patriots. A fellow on one of our dark web message boards said I could leave the trailer at his grain mill.

"From there, we'll find a shallow crossing where we can drive the pickups across the Red River into Oklahoma."

"Couldn't we try to communicate with one of the militias in Oklahoma on a message board and tell them we're coming in? Maybe we could cross over on one of the bridges."

Ulysses shook his head. "It would be a firefight, even if the Oklahoma side knew we were coming and had double the number of troops on the bridge. Somebody would get killed, and that somebody might be you."

"*Somebody* might get killed picking up Chip."

"Don't remind me." Ulysses pursed his lips. "Anyway, it's a calculated risk. Chip has information. He's a high-value target. Left here to his own devices, I'm afraid he'll continue to be a source of worry for us. Getting rid of him is worth the risk.

"The only possible advantage to crossing into Oklahoma by way of a bridge is that we get to bring the trailer and the supplies. I've got plenty of room at the farmhouse, and plenty of supplies. If need be, I can buy another trailer.

"Leaving the trailer in northern Texas could have merit as well. If Foley ever comes back down this way and gets stuck, he'd at least have a place to put his head and something to eat."

Ava did not want to remember that Foley wasn't done fighting. "I understand. It makes sense. You think that section of the river near Byers will be shallow enough to cross with the trucks?"

"I hope so. If not, we'll walk across and hitch a ride home with the militia."

"What if they don't recognize us?"

Ulysses smiled. "If they get a good look past that short black hair, they'll recognize you from the news. Besides, I've been in contact with the Oklahoma militia. They're expecting us to cross over with a big prize for the Alliance States."

"You didn't tell me that."

"Last time I discussed my online relationships with you, it ended in a shootout. Forgive me if I'm not as forthcoming these days."

Ava furrowed her brow but said nothing. It was a sharp jab, but she knew she deserved it. "I'll go check on Charity. I'll see if she thinks she can do it."

"I understand that she's hurting, but I really need her to do this for us." Ulysses nodded. "I also understand that it's a long drive, but Buckley will be with her."

Ava took a deep breath and entered the trailer. She had to make Charity understand the importance of her role.

# CHAPTER 26

Then Moses called Joshua and said to him in the sight of all Israel, "Be strong and of good courage, for you must go with this people to the land which the Lord has sworn to their fathers to give them, and you shall cause them to inherit it. And the Lord, He is the One who goes before you. He will be with you, He will not leave you nor forsake you; do not fear nor be dismayed."

Deuteronomy 31:7-8

Ava woke up late Friday. Partly because it took her a while to go to sleep the night before, and partly because her father had advised her to get as much sleep as possible. He'd warned her that the mission to capture Chip would be a pre-dawn raid, and it would likely be at least 36 hours before she'd have another opportunity to rest.

She began her day with a long hot shower, knowing it could be a couple days before she had another one of those. She returned to the small bedroom of the trailer and got dressed. Charity turned over in the bed. She looked at Ava but said nothing.

"How are you feeling? Did you sleep okay?" Ava sat on the narrow bench to put her boots on.

Charity pulled the comforter up to her chin. "I slept. But not great. I keep dreaming of James. And I don't think I'll ever get that image of him being gunned down out of my mind."

"Do you think you're going to be able to drive the Sierra and the trailer up to the border tonight?"

"I'll do it. I know you need me to."

Ava wished she didn't have to push Charity to take on this task, but there really was no other way. "Thank you. We should be there around 10:00 tomorrow morning, or soon after."

"Why so long? Byers is only five hours away, even if you don't take the interstate."

"We're going to pick him up at around 4:30 in the morning. I'm fairly confident he goes drinking every Friday night so that increases the odds of him being home at that hour. It also means he won't be in much of a position to put up a fight. It's also doubtful that we'll run into very many other people on the way in, or the way out. It's a luxury residential high-rise with mostly young people in the building. Going in the backway bypasses all the security that Chip is likely to have in the lobby. Then, we'll only have to deal with guards at his door."

"It makes sense." Charity sat up in bed. "How are you going to get in?"

"I'll lurk by the exit gate of the parking garage. I'll catch a car leaving, duck inside, then wait for someone to let me in the building while they're going out."

"Sounds risky."

"Not really. I'm a single girl by myself. No one will think anything of it. I'll block the door locks with duct tape and work my way down to the side entrance where I'll let Foley and Dad in. Once we're inside, it'll be easy."

"Be safe. I'm going to be worried until you get to Byers."

"Don't worry for me; pray for me."

"I will."

"Come on. Let's get something to eat. You've got an important job today and a long drive. You need a good breakfast. Plus, I'm counting on you to take care of Buckley."

Charity forced a smile and slowly came out from beneath the covers. "Okay."

That evening, Charity and Buckley left at sunset. Ava, Foley, and Ulysses still had several more hours of waiting at the Buchannan Lake Campground. They reviewed the plan, discussed contingencies, and alternate escape routes. Finally, at 1:00 in the morning, Ulysses did a final gear check on his team. They double checked their radios, which would only be used if the earbuds and mics failed to work on their burner phones. All three of them dressed in civilian clothing. They would blend in perfectly with people coming in from the bars after a hard Friday night of drinking.

For the initial entry, Ava would be armed only with her small Glock 43 tucked in the front of her jeans and covered by her black leather jacket. She'd carry her .45 in her oversized purse, which would also be used to carry out Chip's electronic devices for further inspection.

Foley would have a concealed pistol, and he would bring in the rifles with a large rolling suitcase. Ulysses would trail behind, ready to neutralize anyone who got in the way. Once they arrived on Chip's floor, they'd take out the rifles and be ready for the extraction.

The entry would be very clandestine. The exit, however, would be messy. They'd be carrying at least one hostage, bound and gagged, and they'd be running out of the building with guns blazing. It would be a race against time to get Chip to Foley's truck and get out of Austin before they got caught.

At 3:30 Saturday morning, Ava stood against the back of Chip's high-rise condo building. Her hand was in her purse clutching the grip of her 1911. On one side of her was the door to the stairwell exit. On the other was the gate for the garage exit. She needed someone to leave the building via one of those portals before 4:30 AM, and before security spotted her hanging out by the back doors. She stayed tight with her back to the wall inside a shallow alcove, which hid her from the surveillance camera above her head.

She guessed the temperature to be around 40 degrees, but the occasional wind, which whipped down the alley, sent shivers all through her body.

Time crept by at a glacial pace. She glanced at the time on her burner phone. *4:00 AM. Seems like I've been here for an hour.*

If no one came out by 4:30, Ulysses and Foley would have to use a breaching tool and a sledgehammer to get the metal door open. Even though the door opened to a stairwell, the noise would bring unwanted attention and could jeopardize the mission.

She shuddered from the cold. Suddenly, the door to the stairwell clicked open. An inebriated single guy came out. His delayed reaction first painted his hazy eyes with surprise. As his sluggish brain processed the fact that Ava was a girl, and then a cute girl, a lazy smile grew across his face.

She smiled back. "I lost my key card at the club."

"Hafagreatnight," he slurred.

"Thanks." She pulled the door closed behind her to deter any further interaction with the drunkard.

"I'm in," Ava said over the mic tucked under her jacket. "Let me know when the lush is gone. I'll slap some duct tape over the door lock."

"All clear." Foley waited in his truck, which was parked street side in view of the alley where Ava entered.

She quickly pushed the door open, tore off a length of tape and placed it over the opening in the door frame of the lock. She hustled up the stairs to the second floor. "The interior door to the stairwell has a push bar on the other side. It almost looks like you could jimmy it open with a knife."

Ulysses waited in his truck, which was parked directly behind Foley's. "Can you do it?"

"I don't know. I'm on the second floor. Chip's apartment is on the eighth."

Her father replied, "Head on up there and give it a try. I'm sure I can get it, but a girl jiggling a lock looks like someone who lost her keys. A guy, especially an older man with a scar and a lazy eye, looks like a criminal."

Ava climbed the stairs to the eighth-floor landing. She pulled out her pocket knife and tried. "I don't think I'm going to be able to do it."

"That's okay. Sit tight for a few more minutes. Foley and I will come on in at 4:25."

Ava looked at her phone. "That's fifteen minutes from now. What do I do if someone walks by?"

"You're on the eighth floor. Not many people are going to be trying to get in their cardio by taking the stairs at 4:00 AM on a Saturday morning. Most will take the elevator. But, if someone happens by, give them the same story. You lost your key card. Try to get them to let you in."

"Roger." She waited nervously for the time to pass. She peeked through the rectangular window in the door. Looking down the hall, she spotted two guards sitting in chairs on either side of Chip's door. One was reading a book. The other's thumbs worked frantically at his phone. He was either playing a game or sending a long text. Ava guessed a game was more likely.

She turned back away from the door and relayed the information to Foley and her father.

"Good to know," Ulysses said. "What do they look like? Ex-military?"

"Not at all. They look like Antifa rejects. Undisciplined. Sloppy clothes. Lackadaisical."

"Perfect," he said. "Ten more minutes and we'll be coming to you."

Ava wanted to keep her eye on the guards, but she did not want to risk being spotted. Seconds ticked away like minutes, and minutes like hours.

Finally, Ulysses' voice came over her earbud, "We're on our way. What's going on with the guards?"

Ava took a brief gander through the window. "One of the guards is showing the other one something on his phone."

Minutes later, Ava saw the top of Foley's head coming up the stairs. Next, she saw Ulysses with his short-barreled rifle and silencer ready to fire.

Foley arrived on the eighth-floor landing and unzipped the suitcase. The two AR-15s' uppers and lowers were separated when he removed them from the luggage, but with the click of two small attachment pins on each, he had them reassembled. He handed a rifle to Ava along with a belt, which held four additional magazines. Foley put on a load-bearing vest containing spare magazines for himself and shouldered his rifle.

Ulysses arrived and bent down by the lock. He pulled out his knife and wedged it in the narrow gap between the door and the frame. Click. "Got it.

Foley, bend down and hold this knife in place until I can neutralize the guards."

Ava held Foley's rifle and watched him kneel down to hold the knife. Her heart pounded, knowing the action was about to begin.

Ulysses handed off the knife, drew the butt of his rifle tight against his shoulder and rose slowly. Ava looked through the small window pane from behind her father. The chamber of Ulysses' suppressed rifle snapped open, spitting out a spent shell, making only the sound of the bolt cycling. A loud snap from the bullet passing through the thick glass window caused the second guard to look in Ava's direction. The first guard was already dead. Crack! Glass shards spraying from a second hole in the window of the door was the last thing the second guard would ever see.

"Go," Ulysses instructed.

Foley jerked the door open, folded Uylsses' knife, and handed it back to him. Foley held the door with his foot and took his rifle from Ava's hand as she walked through the doorway. Ulysses led the team down the hall with his rifle up and prepared to fire. Ava trailed behind her father, also with her AR-15 shouldered. Foley took the rear position at the end of the line.

Ulysses quietly approached Chip's door, stepping over the dead guard who lay bleeding on the floor. Ulysses stepped past the second dead watchman on the red-stained hall carpet. He signaled with his hands for Ava to search the guards for the key to Chip's apartment. She slung her rifle around her back and pushed it behind her. Ava bent down and rooted through the first man's pants pocket. She looked at her father and shook her head.

He gestured with his chin to the second guard and she repeated the task. When she located them, Ava held her hands tightly around the keys to keep them from jingling. Ulysses motioned for her to pass them to Foley and get ready to make entry.

Foley moved slowly and deliberately to unlock the deadbolt, then the doorknob. He opened the door in a smooth, even motion. Ulysses walked in first. Ava was next with Foley behind her. Foley locked only the deadbolt once inside.

The soft glow of Chip's floor-to-ceiling fish tank illuminated the kitchen and living space. The soft hum of the pump for the tank's filter helped to conceal the sound of their footsteps. Ava nodded to the bottles near the sink. A bottle of Woodford Reserve Bourbon contained only a few remaining ounces. A bottle of Grey Goose Vodka next to it appeared to be bone dry.

Ulysses nodded and gestured for Foley to lead the way toward the bedroom. Foley reached the bedroom door and opened it. Ulysses and Ava made their way in silently.

Chip lay facing them with his mouth open and tongue hanging out. Raquel slept on the other side of the bed. Ava recognized her by her slender frame covered only by a thin sheet and her short black hair.

Ulysses quietly slung his rifle behind his back and put his arm around the front of Chip's neck. He braced his other arm around the back of Chip's neck, wedging his hand in the elbow joint to put

Chip in a sleeper hold.

Chip began to thrash and kick, trying to free himself from Ulysses' grip. The ruckus awakened Raquel who screamed when she saw Ava's team in the bedroom.

Ulysses continued to apply pressure to Chip's throat. "Foley, get her gagged and bound with duct tape."

Raquel screamed, "No! Please! I'm naked!"

Ulysses' brow wrinkled into deep rows. "Ava, get her a robe. Foley, if she moves, kill her."

Ava quickly searched the bathroom for a robe. She came back and flung it at Raquel. "Put this on and get on the floor. Don't play with us. We will kill you."

Raquel slipped into the robe and then lay down on the floor. "What are you going to do with us?"

Chip's body fell limp in Ulysses' arms. Ulysses rolled him over and began restraining his hands and feet. "Don't worry about that right now. We want your boyfriend. You're extra credit. So, if you make things hard for me, I'll put a bullet in your head and leave you on the floor. Your choice."

Foley finished wrapping Raquel's hands and began running a length of duct tape around her mouth. "Boss, we've got a problem."

Ulysses sighed. "What is it?"

"She's wearing an alarm around her neck." Foley unsnapped the thin metal chain from around Raquel's neck and held up the small alert device.

"Panic button. We need to move!" Ulysses hoisted Chip up onto his shoulder. "Ava, find Chip's laptop and phone and stick them in your purse. Keep your rifle ready to fire. Foley, you go out first. Keep the girl in front and use her as a shield. Press your rifle against her head. If she gives you anything less than 110% compliance, drop her. I doubt she can tell us anything that Chip can't. She's expendable."

"Roger." Foley lifted Raquel off the floor and pushed her with his rifle. "Move! To the stairs. Slow and steady."

Ava found Chip's phone on the nightstand and stuck it in her bag. She located his laptop on the coffee table. That was also quickly stowed away in the large purse. She spun it around to her back and readied her rifle.

"Keep moving!" Ulysses held Chip over his left shoulder and gripped his rifle with his right hand.

Ava filed out of the apartment behind Foley and Raquel. She looked down at the footprints of blood being put down by Raquel who may or may not have intentionally walked through the puddles outside the door. "We're not going to be hard to track." She gestured toward the prints of Raquel's feet.

Gunfire erupted from the hallway intersection, in the direction of the elevator. Ulysses grunted, "It won't matter now."

Foley yelled. "Ten hostiles, incoming." He pushed Raquel to the ground, then took a knee and returned fire.

"Can you hold 'em back until we get to the stairs?" Ulysses asked.

"Roger!" Foley continued to fire.

Ulysses looked at Ava. "When I say go, you run

for that door. Hold it open for me."

"Got it!"

"Go!"

Ava ran past the intersection while Foley laid down suppressive fire.

"Hold your fire! I've got your boss hostage over here. You'll kill him if you shoot." Ulysses yelled before running. He positioned Chip's limp form to be between his head and the gunfire before running across. POW, POW, POW! Still, the hostiles fired at Ulysses when he crossed the intersection.

Ulysses reached the stairwell unharmed. He looked at Ava. "This bunch is out of hand. They don't seem to care if they kill Chip. We have no leverage. We've gotta move. Foley, we'll cover you. Send the girl first, then come to us."

"Roger." Foley lifted Raquel by the scruff of her robe and pushed her toward the door. He sent another volley of bullets down the hall and turned to run.

Raquel's eyes showed her deep distress as she ran with her mouth gagged and her hands bound behind her back toward the stairwell.

POP! POP! POW, POW! POP! Gunfire echoed off the walls of the hallway.

Ava watched while a splatter of blood exploded from Foley's shin. He continued to run to the door, then collapsed in pain once he reached the stairwell landing. Foley quickly rolled over and began shooting at the hostiles who'd rounded the corner. From the cover of the door frame, Foley, Ava, and Ulysses gunned down four hostiles, sending the others back around the corner for cover.

Ulysses dropped Chip to the floor. He looked at Raquel with blazing eyes. "These people have no problem killing you either. I should blow your brains out right here and right now for pushing that button." He raised the butt of his rifle and slammed it against Raquel's head, knocking her out and sending her to the ground. Ulysses bent down to look at Foley's leg. "Is it bad?"

"It's bad, sir." Foley changed magazines.

"I'll help you down the stairs." Ava put her arm under Foley's shoulder.

He pulled away. "You can't carry my weight. Especially down eight flights of stairs."

Ava looked at Ulysses. "Then Dad will carry you down. We'll leave Chip here."

Foley shook his head. "Somebody has to hold the other six off so you can get down the stairs. And you have to go now. They'll be all over the exit if you don't leave right this instant."

"I'm not leaving you, Foley!" Ava was shocked at what he was suggesting.

"You have to. I love you, Ava." He took her hand for a brief second. He put his thumb and index finger on the homemade ring around her finger. "I'll always love you. But you have to go. Now!"

Ava's heart stopped beating. The blood drained from her face. Paralyzing fear rushed through her capillaries causing the surface of her skin to feel like it was burning. "No!" She gasped for air and turned to her father. "Dad! Tell him!"

Ulysses' face revealed his resignation to the unthinkable. "He's right, Ava. We have to go. And someone has to hold them off."

She shook her head, pleading with Foley. She sobbed, "Please don't do this! I need you. I love you." She grabbed his hand.

"I know. And I love you, too. But you have to go right now." He gently pulled his hand away from hers.

"I can't leave you. I won't!"

"You have to. You have to now. I'll always love you." Foley broke his gaze into Ava's eyes. He turned away and took aim. He prepared to spend his final breaths holding off the enemy so Ava could get away.

"Come on." Ulysses hoisted Chip back upon his shoulder. "We have to go." He let his rifle hang from the sling and tugged Ava away by the back of her jacket.

"No!" She cried as she reluctantly began to descend the stairs.

"I know, baby. I know. Just keep going." Ulysses was behind her, hurrying her along.

Ava reached the sixth floor, her body wracked with grief and horror. She heard the exchange of gunfire above her.

"We have to move fast, Ava. You have to keep moving." Ulysses coached her.

She wailed as she reached the lower floors and the reality of what just happened set in. The rifle fire from above became more muffled.

"Stop when you get to the bottom," Ulysses said. "If we have trouble outside, you'll run to the truck with my keys and start the engine. I'll use Chip as a shield and lay down cover fire while I run to the truck. If I get hit, just go. Meet up with Charity like we planned. Cross over to Oklahoma. You've got the address to my place. You and Charity take care of each other. That's all I want. That's all Foley would want."

Ava couldn't believe this was happening. This was supposed to be a simple abduction. How had this plan turned so terribly wrong? "No, Daddy! Don't say that!" She continued to bawl.

They reached the exit door. Ulysses let his rifle hang and pulled the keys out of his pocket. He handed them to Ava. "You remember the plan, right?"

She took the keys and nodded, unable to formulate words over her sobbing.

"On my count." Ulysses adjusted the weight of Chip's body on his shoulder, then positioned his rifle. "Three, two, one, GO!"

Ava threw all of her anger and rage against the door, throwing it open and slamming it against the outside wall. She charged toward the pickup while two black Humvees screeched to a halt. SJL soldiers armed with AK-47s poured out of each. Bang, Bang, Bang! POW, POW, POW! Gunfire erupted all around her.

She thought of nothing but getting to the truck. Her legs filled with adrenaline. She pumped her feet against the pavement, the bag and rifle slapping against her back with each stride. She reached the pickup and spun around to see SJL fighters trying to shoot Ulysses without hitting Chip.

She leveled her rifle on the hood of the truck for cover and began firing. POP! POP! POP! Two of the soldiers fell to the ground. POW! POW! Ulysses dropped one more. He continued rushing toward the vehicle. He let Chip roll off his shoulder into the bed of the truck. "Get in and drive!" he shouted.

Ava emptied her magazine on the assailants before complying, but eventually opened the door and started the engine.

Ulysses rolled down his window and fired upon the remaining SJL soldiers while Ava drove off. "Take Lamar north out of town. It's 4:45 in the morning. Hopefully, not many people are on the road. Run the red lights."

"Wouldn't it be safer to take I-35 or the expressway?" She checked the rearview.

"They'll be looking for us there. This is our best shot at getting out of town. And turn off your headlights."

"Run red lights with no lights on? This is suicide!"

"We'll be harder to tail with no lights. Just for the first couple miles. Once I'm sure we're not being followed and no helicopters are after us, you can turn them back on."

Ava glanced over at her father. "You're bleeding. Your stomach!"

Ulysses looked down. "Must have got grazed."

"Is it bad?"

"No. Superficial."

"Are you telling me the truth?"

"Yes, Ava. I won't lie to you, even to save your feelings. If I was in bad shape, I'd want to spend my final moments saying goodbye; not covering up the inevitable."

Her brows pressed together. She was still

horrified at having left Foley to die. It was an event she might never get over.

"Once we get out of town, we'll have to check the one in the back for leaks."

"I hope he bleeds out. No. I hope he's still alive so I can kill him when we pull over."

"I'm angry, too. But we have to keep him alive. Otherwise, Foley's sacrifice will have been in vain."

She checked the rearview once more. Seeing no one behind her, Ava's fear and anxiety slowly gave way to sorrow and a broken heart.

Seconds later, Ulysses said, "We've got company."

She glanced again to see a pair of headlights behind her. They appeared to belong to a large vehicle. "Is that one of the Hummers?"

"I think so. Go as fast as you can."

Fright and terror returned, clouding out the sadness. "What should I do? Turn off onto a side street?"

"No. We could get trapped. I don't know these back streets. Just keep going until I tell you to slow down." Ulysses pulled one of the bricks of explosives from beneath the seat.

Ava looked long enough to see that it was covered in nails and marbles.

"Okay, pull to the side of the road." Ulysses held the brick in one hand and the detonator in the other.

"Then what?"

"When I say go, punch it all the way to the floor!"

Ava nervously complied.

The Hummer quickly caught up with them and stopped behind them. Three fighters came out the side doors and approached Ava's vehicle with their rifles up.

Ulysses flung the brick out the window toward the back of the truck. Ava watched in what seemed like slow motion as the device spun in the air. She saw it come perilously close to landing in the bed of the truck next to Chip. The explosive hit the tailgate, bounced off, and fell to the ground behind the truck.

"Go!" Ulysses yelled.

She slammed the gas pedal to the floor, causing the tires to spin and smoke as the truck gradually caught traction and sped away. She watched the side view mirror when her father pushed the button of the detonator.

BOOOM!!! Fire and shrapnel quickly caught up with the SJL combatants who tried with futility to jump out of harm's way.

Blazing through intersections and blowing past red lights, she didn't let her foot off the pedal for three miles.

"I think we've lost them." Ulysses had been turned toward the rear of the vehicle. He faced front. "You can turn your lights back on now."

Ava breathed a little easier, but the sense of loss still sat on her like a lead weight. She wondered what Foley's last moments were like. She prayed silently asking God that He would retroactively spare Foley from the pain. She asked Him for strength to keep going, to live a life worthy of the sacrifice Foley had made. Ava knew in her heart that she would never ever love another man the way she'd loved Foley. And she was certain she'd never forget him.

Three days later was Christmas Eve. Ava had not been out of bed since the remnants of the team arrived at her father's farm in northeastern Oklahoma. Buckley had remained by her side, except to go eat or to go outside to do his business. But it was time to get up. Like it or not, she had to get on with life.

Ava forced herself to get out of bed. Charity was still mourning her loss, but she'd found the strength to pitch in. She did laundry, washed dishes, and fed the chickens.

As much as Ava's heart hurt over the loss of Foley, she would not let herself sink beyond the point of no return. If she did, that would mean that Markovich had won. It would mean that Foley's death had been in vain.

She walked into the kitchen and poured herself a cup of cold coffee. She didn't bother reheating it. She drank it cold. She opened the cupboards to look for something to eat.

Ulysses came in the back door, walked to the kitchen sink and washed his hands. "How are you feeling?"

She toyed with the homemade engagement ring on her finger. "Not good. Not good at all. But I'm not going to sit around and feel sorry for myself. I'm going to town today. I have to get some hair color. I can't keep looking at this person with the short black hair in the mirror. It sounds stupid, but getting my hair back to normal is important."

He dried his hands on the towel hanging from the handle on the stove. "If you're going to town, you should go soon. It's Christmas Eve. Lots of places will be closing early.

"But it's not stupid to want to fix your hair. You need to mourn. And you need to feel like yourself to do that."

Her father had articulated her feelings very well. She appreciated his ability to understand. "Once that's out of the way, I want to help out around here. Tell me what you need me to do, and I'll try to do my share."

"That's a good attitude, but give yourself time to grieve. The pain won't go away, but it will become manageable. You can't rush it. Time takes time."

She swallowed hard, intent on not breaking down right now. She pulled a box of bakery mix from the shelf. "How about some biscuits?"

"That will be fine. If you're up for it, I'll eat some with you. But like I said, don't push yourself."

Ava put the box next to the sink and found a bowl to mix the ingredients. "Did Chip give you any information yet?"

Ulysses rolled his sleeves down. "He gave me his computer password in exchange for eight hours of sleep. But so far that's it. I'm in no hurry. If I can avoid torture, I will. Extracting information like that has its toll on the interrogator. It costs you part of who you are. I've spent a good amount of that already.

"Anyway, he's not a true believer. The impression I get is that Chip was in it for the money and the power. After a couple days of nothing but water, he'll be ready to trade Szabos' location for a ham sandwich."

She preheated the oven. "You think he knows where George Szabos is?"

"Yeah. He's probably not in the country, but Chip will tell me the location of whoever is serving as his lieutenant."

Ava decided to simply spoon the biscuits out on a sheet pan rather than rolling them out. "I bet it's Shane Lawrence. He'll be hard to get to."

"Yeah. But anyone can be gotten to. Besides that, Chip knows all about the flow of weapons and supplies to the Social Justice Legion. If the Alliance States can disrupt Markovich's logistics network, that information will really make a difference."

"But you won't get involved in the actual fighting, right?" She finished spooning the dough onto the pan.

"I told you, Ava. I'm not going to leave your side; not ever again."

She took comfort in her father's words. Ava slid the pan into the oven. Her phone vibrated in her pocket. She took it out. "Seems like that text forwarder you set up for me is working. I just got a message on my burner phone from my old number."

"Even though we're out of enemy territory, they could still track us down with your old phone. Who's the message from?"

Ava opened the text. "Raquel."

"What does it say?"

She read it aloud. "Seems like we got our boyfriends mixed up. Wanna trade?" She looked up at her father with hopeful eyes.

He shook his head slowly. "Don't fall into her trap, Ava. Ask her for proof that he's alive."

Ava shot a message back via an encrypted email-to-text app over Orfox, the mobile Tor browser on her phone. She stared anxiously at the screen and waited. Seconds later, she showed her father the picture of Foley tied to a chair, but very much alive. Joy sprung up from inside her, overflowing through tears of jubilation.

Ulysses smiled as he hugged her. "Congratulations, sweetie. Looks like I'm going to have to get to work on Chip. We may not have him for as long as I thought."

Ava's sorrow and the torment of her soul faded. Where only despair had been, hope flourished. She knew getting Foley back wouldn't be easy, but with the help of her earthly father and her Heavenly Father, all things were possible.

Her days of worry were far from over. But if she could hold Foley in her arms for just one more day, it was an amicable compromise. The flicker of hope from that remote possibility was the best Christmas present she could ask for.

# DON'T PANIC!

Inevitably, books like this will wake folks up to the need to be prepared, or cause those of us who are already prepared to take inventory of our preparations. New preppers can find the task of getting prepared for an economic collapse, EMP, or societal breakdown to be a source of great anxiety. It shouldn't be. By following an organized plan and setting a goal of getting a little more prepared each day, you can do it.

I always try to include a few prepper tips in my novels, but they're fiction and not a comprehensive plan to get prepared. Now that you're motivated to start prepping, the last thing I want to do is leave you frustrated, not knowing what to do next. So I'd like to offer you a free PDF copy of *The Seven Step Survival Plan.*

For the new prepper, *The Seven Step Survival Plan* provides a blueprint that prioritizes the different aspects of preparedness and breaks them down into achievable goals. For seasoned preppers who often get overweight in one particular area of preparedness, *The Seven Step Survival Plan* provides basic guidelines to help keep their plan in balance, and ensures they're not missing any critical segments of a well-adjusted survival strategy.

To get your **FREE** copy of ***The Seven Step Survival Plan***, go to **PrepperRecon.com** and click the FREE PDF banner, just below the menu bar, at the top of the home page.

Thank you for reading
***Ava's Crucible, Book Two:***
***Embers of Empire***

Reviews are the best way to help get the book noticed. If you liked the book, please take a moment to leave a five-star review on Amazon and Goodreads.

I love hearing from readers! So whether it's to say you enjoyed the book, to point out a typo that we missed, or asked to be notified when new books are released, drop me a line.
**prepperrecon@gmail.com**

Stay tuned to **PrepperRecon.com** for the latest news about my upcoming books, and great interviews on the **Prepper Recon Podcast**.


Continue the adventure with
***Ava's Crucible, Book Three:***
***United We Stand***

If you've enjoyed Ava's Crucible, you'll love my end-times thriller series, ***The Days of Noah***

Tennessee public school teacher, Noah Parker, like many in the United States, has been asleep at the wheel. During his complacency, the founding precepts of America have been slowly, systematically destroyed by a conspiracy that dates back hundreds of years.

Cassandra Parker, Noah's wife, has diligently followed end-times prophecy and the shifting tide against freedom in America. Noah has tried to avoid the subject, but when charges are filed against him for deviating from the approved curriculum in his school, he quickly understands the seriousness of the situation. The signs can no longer be ignored, and Noah is forced to prepare for the cataclysmic period of financial and political upheaval ahead.

Meanwhile, in an off-site CIA facility outside of Langley, rookie analyst Everett Carroll discovers he's not being told the whole truth. He's instructed to disregard troubling information uncovered by his research. Everett ignores his directive and keeps digging. What he finds goes against everything he's been taught to believe. Unfortunately, his curiosity doesn't escape the attention of his superiors, and it may cost him his life.

Watch through the eyes of Noah Parker and Everett Carroll as the world descends into chaos, a global empire takes shape, ancient writings are fulfilled, and the last days fall upon the once-great United States of America.

If you have an affinity for the prophetic don't miss my EMP survival series, ***Seven Cows, Ugly and Gaunt***

In ***Book One: Behold Darkness and Sorrow***, Daniel Walker begins having prophetic dreams about the judgment coming upon America for rejecting God. Through one of his dreams, Daniel learns of an imminent threat of an EMP attack which will wipe out America's electric grid and most all computerized devices, sending the country into a technological dark age.

Living in a nation where all life-sustaining systems of support are completely dependent on electricity and computers, the odds for survival are dismal. Municipal water services, retail food distribution, police, fire, EMS and all emergency services will come to a screeching halt.

If they want to live, Daniel and his friends must focus on faith, wits and preparation to be ready . . . before the lights go out.

You'll also enjoy my first series,

## *The Economic Collapse Chronicles*

The series begins with *Book One: American Exit Strategy*. Matt and Karen Bair thought they were prepared for anything, but can they survive a total collapse of the economic system? If they want to live through the crisis, they'll have to think fast and move quickly. In a world where all the rules have changed, and savagery is law, those who hesitate pay with their very lives.

When funds are no longer available for government programs, widespread civil unrest erupts across the country. Matt and Karen are forced to move to a more remote location and their level of preparedness is revealed as being much less adequate than they believed prior to the crisis. Civil instability erupts into civil war and Americans are forced to choose a side. Don't miss this action-packed, post-apocalyptic tale about survival after the total collapse of America.

# ABOUT THE AUTHOR

Mark Goodwin is a Christian constitutional author and the host of the popular Prepper Recon Podcast which interviews patriots, preppers, and economists each week on PrepperRecon.com to help people prepare for the coming storm. Mark holds a degree in accounting and monitors macro-economic conditions to stay up-to-date with the ongoing global meltdown. He is an avid student of the Holy Bible and spends several hours every week devoted to the study of Scripture and the prophecies contained therein. The troubling trends in the moral, social, political, and financial landscapes have prompted Mark to conduct extensive research within the arena of preparedness. He weaves his knowledge of biblical prophecy, economics, politics, prepping, and survival into an action-packed tapestry of post-apocalyptic fiction. Having been a sinner saved by grace himself, the story of redemption is a prominent theme in all of Mark's writings.

"He brought me up also out of an horrible pit, out of the miry clay, and set my feet upon a rock, and established my goings."
Psalm 40:2

81932860R00160

Made in the USA
San Bernardino, CA
12 July 2018